GAME TIME
DECISION

Game Time Decision

Brooklyn Monarchs, Book V

PATRICIA SARGEANT

Mediopolis Communications, LLC

Contents

DEDICATION

To my dream team:
* My sister, Bernadette, for giving
me the dream.
* My husband, Michael, for
supporting the dream.
* My brother Richard for believing
in the dream.
* My brother Gideon for
encouraging the dream.
And to Mom and Dad, always with
love.

Chapter 1

"You can't be serious."

Zerleena Chase's wide-eyed stare and offended tone weren't the reactions Marlon Burress had expected when he'd said he wanted to marry her.

"I *am* serious." And very, very confused.

He lowered his flute of red wine and studied her heart-shaped brown features, looking for a reason for her scathing response. Maybe she was tired? Ill? Had the wine gone straight to her head?

After all these years, he hadn't thought his college sweetheart would throw herself across the table and into his arms. But he hadn't expected her scorn, either. He'd assumed she'd at least consider his proposal. Instead she'd shut him down with deflating speed and determination like Hakeem Olajuwan, the seven-foot retired professional basketball center, blocking shots at the post.

Maybe she hadn't understood him. He repeated the words. "Let's get married."

Zerleena's caramel gaze dipped to his half-full wine flute before lifting again to search his eyes. "How much did you have to drink before dinner?"

"I'm not drunk, Leena. And I'm not kidding." Why was she acting like this? Was she in shock?

"Did you hit your head on your way over here?" Zerleena's dry declaration puzzled him.

Shaking his head, Marlon turned away, taking a moment to gather his thoughts.

The Italian restaurant in downtown Brooklyn, New York, was full, a testament to its popularity. Its dark wood and crimson red décor gave the establishment a warm, romantic feel. The air was heavy with the aroma of rich sauces and generous seasonings. Each table was dressed with a crisp white tablecloth and a slim, crystal vase, presenting a single deep red rose.

He patted himself on the back for picking the perfect spot for a wedding proposal. DeMarcus Guinn, his former teammate and long-time friend — and now that he was playing for the Brooklyn Monarchs, his head coach — had recommended it.

Marlon had felt the stares from the other Saturday evening guests. As a two-time National Basketball Association champion and former league Most Valuable Player, he was used to the attention. Fans of his previous franchise, Florida's Miami Waves, had been intense. Brooklyn Monarchs fans weren't as enthusiastic about him. Yet. But their attention this evening was proof they were warming up. He ignored their stares tonight, though. Tonight was all about Zerleena. She hadn't noticed the looks or at least she hadn't said anything.

Marlon returned his attention to his date; his future wife, once she realized he was serious. She was texting again. "Leena, we were good together."

"*Were*. In college. *Fifteen*. Years. Ago." Zerleena spaced her words as though driving home the history. She set her cell phone aside.

"You look even better now. You've been working out." Marlon offered her a hopeful half smile.

Zerleena at twenty-two had been sexy. Zerleena at thirty-seven was hot as hell. Her raven hair was shorter. It framed her face and swung above her narrow shoulders. Her soft, generous curves had firmed. There was a maturity in her wide caramel eyes that hadn't been there in college. Perhaps there also was a touch of cynicism, which seemed to be directed at him. It challenged and excited him.

Her gaze cooled, causing Marlon's smile to shrivel and die. Hope stood on shaky ground.

"I haven't heard from you since we graduated. Once you were drafted to the NBA, you broke up with me. Do you remember? I do. You said a relationship would cramp your new lifestyle."

That was then. "Things are different now."

Her eyes flared again before narrowing. "How?"

Marlon leaned into the table, willing her to understand. "I've been traded to the Monarchs. We're in the same city—"

"With more than eight million other people."

"— And since I'll be retiring soon, this would be a good time for me to consider settling down, maybe even raising a family."

Zerleena's lips parted. She gave him a slow blink. "Start a family *with whom*?"

Marlon smiled, inclining his head toward her. "With you."

"Hold on, pal." Zerleena extended her right hand, palm out. "I haven't heard from you in *fifteen* years. Not five. Not ten. *Fifteen*. And now because you've moved into my city you assume my ovaries are happy to see you? They're not."

Marlon leaned back against his chair. She'd scrambled his thoughts. He hadn't expected such fierce opposition from her. He hadn't anticipated any opposition at all. He hadn't planned for them. He'd expected her to be glad to see him; happy to get back together. They'd been in love.

He started to speak, but their server materialized beside their table. Had the young woman overheard any of Zerleena's takedown? He hoped not.

Their server gave Zerleena a shy smiled. "Is there anything else I can get for you, Ms. Chase?"

How did she know Leena's name? Marlon didn't recall an introduction.

Zerleena's smile for the young woman was warmer than any she'd given him all evening. In fact, she hadn't smiled at him at all. "Just our checks, please. Everything has been wonderful and I'm ready to leave. Thank you, Nev."

"You're welcome, Ms. Chase." Nev's cheeks turned pink when Zerleena said her name.

Surprised, Marlon frowned at the young woman beside him. How had Zerleena known her name? For the first time, he noticed the server's nametag. Sighing, he switched his attention back to his date. She still hadn't used his name. "Pal" was the most personal address she'd given him since they'd reconnected almost three weeks ago.

He held up a hand. "One check, please."

"*Two* checks, please, Nev. *Two*." Smiling, Zerleena held up two fingers as though emphasizing her request. Her tone didn't invite further discussion.

"Of course, Ms. Chase." Nev nodded at Marlon before leaving.

He took a deep breath, drawing in the scents of oregano and cheese, and preparing to reengage in a battle he hadn't expected. "I've never forgotten you, Leena."

"I might have believed that — *if* you'd stayed in touch."

"Don't you think what we had in college is worth recapturing?"

Zerleena's eyes hardened. "If *you* didn't think our relationship was worth keeping, why would *I* think it's worth rekindling?"

Heat crawled up his neck and into his face. They both knew he didn't have an answer for that. "But you accepted my dinner invitation."

"It was the only way to get you to stop blowing up my home phone." Zerleena's expression was a mixture of frustration and disgruntlement. "I should file a complaint against the university's alumni office for giving you my number."

"You selected the option to allow classmates to reconnect with you." They'd met move-in day their first year and had been together for the next four.

"That was meant for everyone *but* you. It's my fault for not specifying that. I'd never wanted to hear from you again. I thought you felt the same way."

She'd drawn blood with that last arrow. He filled his lungs to ease the tightness in his chest. "Did my leaving really hurt you that badly?"

"*Yes.*"

He heard the strain in the hissed word; saw her struggle to remain calm. How did he respond to that? Did she even want a reply? Marlon dropped his eyes from her scorching glare.

Nev's reappearance was a welcome reprieve. She delivered their separate checks, and took their plates and silverware.

"Thank you." Zerleena's gratitude didn't even hint at the anger she'd blasted Marlon with seconds before. It was an impressive display of the poise and confidence she'd developed since college. She handed Nev her credit card.

Marlon did the same. Alone again, he reached for his wine flute. "When we were in college, you always insisted on splitting the check."

Zerleena responded with a stony stare. She snatched her cell again. Who was she texting? She wouldn't tell him even if he asked.

Undaunted Marlon continued. "There's no one else, Leena."

"I don't care about your private life, pal."

He winced. She refused to use his name. "It's true that I'm not dating. But I wasn't talking about me."

Zerleena's cheeks flushed. Was it anger or embarrassment? "What makes you think I'm not in a relationship?"

Nev interrupted again, this time with their cards and receipts. She thanked them for coming and wished them a good evening before vanishing for the last time.

Marlon slipped his card into his wallet. "If you'd really wanted me to stop calling, you could've told me you were seeing someone – whether or not that was true." He pinned her with a look. "I think a part of you wanted to see me again, if only to satisfy your curiosity."

"What would I be curious about?" Zerleena returned her wallet to her purse.

"Whether I still have any effect on you." He arched an eyebrow. "Do I?"

Zerleena stood. "I see you're still lugging around that ego, pal." She'd spent the entire evening with him without once saying his name.

Marlon noted her stiff gait as he followed her across the restaurant. She didn't want to admit there was still something between them. He didn't have that issue. He was still drawn to Zerleena, perhaps more now than in college. Twenty-something Leena had been sweet and, yes, adoring. Ms. Chase would make a man work for the pleasure of her attention. Marlon could never turn down a challenge.

How can I convince her to give me another chance?

***

How can I convince him to stay away from me?

Zerleena knew she'd drawn the attention of the restaurant's other guests as she crossed the hardwood flooring toward the front doors Saturday evening. She was used to it. Usually she ignored the stares. Tonight, she didn't want any witnesses if she lost control and started screaming at Marlon like a woman possessed.

Fifteen.

Years.

Her fuming internal voice warned her to remain calm. But her mind played a fantasy loop of her slugging him in the middle of this expensive Italian restaurant, knocking him on his still-too-fine behind.

Fifteen.

Years.

Keep it together, Leena.

She made a conscious effort to keep her hands unfisted and her back straight as she placed one foot in front of the other.

Zerleena inclined her head toward the restaurant's hostess. Based on the young woman's gushy smile and enthusiastic wave, she must have read her personal finance management books, listened to her satellite radio program, or attended her workshops. Possibly all three. Zerleena gave her a warm smile before leading Marlon through the doors.

"I'll take you home." His voice was far too close —
and his words way too presumptuous.

"No. Thank you." Zerleena tightened the belt of
her pale peach cotton-blend coat against the biting
mid-October breeze. She blamed her trembling on the
weather rather than his nearness. Her body wouldn't
betray her like that.

Would it?

The scents of the saucy, spicy entrees from the
restaurant behind them along with the aroma of pas-
tries from a nearby bakery, and automobile exhaust
from the bottlenecked traffic on the boulevard in
front of them carried on the evening air. A weird com-
bination, but that was life in New York.

Marlon gave her his crooked smile. The one that
used to make her toes curl. The one that was making
her toes curl right now.

What was wrong with her?

"Afraid you won't be able to resist me?" He still
knew the buttons to push.

Beneath the exhaust fumes, Zerleena smelled the
trap he'd set. "Not at all." She gave him a scathing
once over – and almost swallowed her tongue. His behind wasn't the only thing that was still fine.

She'd watched enough of the Miami Waves' tele-
vised games to know the years had been kind to him,
much to her annoyance. Marlon on television was one
thing, though. Remove the distance and Marlon in
person was an event one had to prepare for in advance.
Her eyes moved over his close-cropped hair, warm

brown skin, chiseled features, full lips, and wide ebony eyes. His broad shoulders under his lightweight topcoat were a dangerous distraction. The early autumn breeze wasn't enough to cool her body's reaction to his blatant sex appeal.

"Then let me take you home. My car's over there." Marlon nodded toward a parking lot across the street. He tossed out the invitation as though her response didn't matter, but his negligent tone clashed with the watchful look in his eyes.

Zerleena strained to resist his baiting. "My driver's on her way."

She searched the traffic. *Where was Millicent? She should be here by now. New York traffic. Urgh.*

"Is that who you were texting in the restaurant?"

"Yes." She didn't care that he'd noticed her rudeness.

"You should've told me. I'm glad to take you home."

"I don't want you to know where I live."

She scanned the street again. *Come on. Come on.*

Marlon shrugged but his eyes darkened with disappointment. "Suit yourself. I can understand if you find me too irresistible to be in close quarters with for any length of time."

"What an ego." Zerleena struggled to keep her voice down, conscious of the crowds moving past them on the streets of the city that never sleeps. "No matter what you think, you're *not* irresistible."

"Prove it. Cancel your driver and let me take you home." Marlon's eyes gleamed above her.

Is he laughing at me? She gave a wordless growl. "You're an impossible man."

"And you're an incredibly beautiful woman."

Zerleena caught her breath. Her mind scolded her. *Slow down, girlfriend. Those are just words. They'd've meant more if his actions hadn't been so shitty.*

Her heart betrayed her. *True, but he'd never used them so well.*

"Save your sonnets, Shakespeare." Zerleena kept her eyes on the traffic. "I'm not cancelling my driver."

Marlon spoke after a beat of silence. His voice was low and pensive, luring her attention back to him. "Thanks for having dinner with me, Leena. It was good to see you again. It brought back a lot of great memories."

Darn you, yes it did. Memories that were the reason your breaking up with me had hurt so much.

Why hadn't I been good enough for you, Marl?

Butterflies circled her stomach. She'd felt this way before. When she'd been an undergrad dating her university's basketball star. She'd boxed those feelings and buried them in the back of her heart. Or so she'd thought. How had they managed to escape?

"Whatever we had died a decade and a half ago." Zerleena held his eyes. "After tonight, there's no reason for us to communicate ever again."

Marlon stepped closer, close enough for her to feel the warmth of his body and the tug of shared memories. In his eyes, she read a question and an answer.

Saw their past and his certainty. He lowered his head toward her.

Zerleena wanted to step back. She needed to step back. She would step back. Any minute now. Her heart was weakening — but her mind was firm.

Her right arm shot out in reflex and self-preservation, pressing hard against his left shoulder and demanding her space. The movement snapped her out of her trance. "Fifteen years. You don't get to pick up where you left off."

A car pulled to the curb beside her. Recognizing it and her driver, Zerleena breathed a sigh of relief. She dropped her arm, fisting her hand to keep its shaking from spreading to the rest of her body. She turned her back to Marlon, shutting him out of her mind — or at least trying to. Without waiting for her driver to get out of the car, Zerleena jerked open the back passenger door and sank onto the seat.

She met her driver's startled eyes in the rearview mirror. "Thank you, Millicent."

Saturday night traffic in downtown Brooklyn meant it would take some time for her driver to maneuver away from the curb. Zerleena smothered a sigh, closed her eyes, and said a silent goodbye to Marlon and their bittersweet past.

Chapter 2

"Leena, girl, you've *got* to explain *this*." Keysha Yardell slapped a copy of the *New York Horn* onto the kitchen table.

Keysha, an attorney with the New York City Law Department, had folded the local paper open to the social page. There, prominently displayed, was an enormous picture of Marlon and Zerleena.

The full-color photo had been taken Saturday evening. They were standing beside her driver's car. The photographer had captured them in the moment she'd stopped Marlon from kissing her. Zerleena could still feel his chest, warm and firm, against her palm. His scent had surrounded her. She took a long drink of the cranberry juice their host had served and told herself to just breathe.

"Hmmm." Erika Franklin, their mutual friend and this week's host of the trio's Sunday brunch, leaned over from the other side of her small square blonde wood kitchen table. She spun the newspaper around for a better look at the tell-all image. "Very nice." She nodded, then returned to the stove.

The photo's headline read: Money Guru's NFL Move Blocks NBA Star's Pass. The caption explained she and Marlon had dined at the Italian Bread before the Monarchs' newest player had tried — and failed — to kiss the finance management queen good-night.

The pricey eatery was a mecca for high-profile figures in and around Brooklyn. That's why the paparazzi were drawn to it — and one of the reasons Zerleena tended to avoid it. She should have done so last night.

"I've seen it and explained it to my parents."

Ramone and Jillian Chase, had been delirious for her. The basketball fanatics were convinced Marlon had never married because he still loved their little girl. It's possible Zerleena had perhaps led them to believe she and Marlon had come to a mutual decision to part ways. Yes, that had been her pride talking.

Zerleena swept aside the newspaper as though she didn't care, but her gaze lingered on Marlon, standing in profile to the camera. The photo didn't do him justice.

"Now you can explain it to us." Keysha returned her newspaper to her oversized crimson handbag.

Erika set their entrées in front of them. "First grace, then you can do your cross examination, counselor. I'm hungry." Erika's Trinidadian roots were evident in the cadence of her command.

Zerleena's smile expressed her gratitude for the food and the rescue. "Erika, this looks wonderful and smells fantastic. Thank you so much."

Her eyes devoured the callaloo, fish bake, and hardo bread arranged on the floral print porcelain plate. The spicy aromas mingled with the scents of strong coffee and freshly baked bread. She recognized the traditional West Indian food from her frequent patronage of Erika's restaurant, Manny's Caribbean Cuisine, named for her friend's late husband.

"It really does look great, Erika. Thank you." Keysha pulled the plate closer to her as she slipped the restauranteur a sly smile. "I still think you should host our brunches every week."

Their host harrumphed. "I cook for other people five days a week. Once in a while, I want someone to cook for me." She arched an eyebrow. "And I mean a meal, Key. Oatmeal doesn't qualify."

Zerleena chuckled. "Erika's right, Key. I still can't believe you tried to get away with serving us oatmeal for brunch.

"I hadn't gotten to the store." Beneath the defensive notes of Keysha's response, Zerleena heard amusement. One of the many things she loved about the other woman was her ability to laugh at herself.

They joined hands as Erika led the prayer over their food. The three of them had met almost twelve years earlier during a financial self-help workshop. The weekend-long event hadn't been worth the registration, but their friendship was priceless. They'd been there for each other through marriages, miscarriage, divorce, and death.

Erika's kitchen reflected her warmth and vitality. The wealth of natural light made the orange, red, and white décor appear even richer. The wide white and red marbled countertops were pristine.

Zerleena dug into her brunch. The buttery, well-season fish bake made her taste buds dance. She reached for her tall glass of juice. Truth be told, she wouldn't be disappointed if Erika chose to host all their brunches in the future. Her friend was a magician in the kitchen.

"So?" Keysha gave Zerleena an expectant look.

Zerleena was tempted to feign confusion, but that kind of subterfuge wouldn't fly with her friends.

She took a bracing drink from her mug of ginger tea. "Marlon's been asking me to get together ever since the Monarchs announced his trade from the Miami Waves."

Keysha exchanged a look with Erika. She was familiar with their expressions. She'd exchanged similar ones with each of them in the past. It signaled her friends' protective antennas had been deployed.

"He knew *you* weren't going to call *him*." Erika swallowed a forkful of the callalou.

Keysha frowned. "Why didn't you tell us?"

Her gaze slipped from the other woman's. "It's not a big deal. And I've had other things on my mind." Did she sound nonchalant enough?

Keysha gave an incredulous laugh. "Leena, the man who broke your heart fourteen years ago—"

"Fifteen," Zerleena corrected. "It was fifteen years ago." Fifteen years, four months, one week, and one day. Zerleena froze. Her subconscious had kept count.

Darn it! And darn him!

"OK. Fifteen." Keysha set down her fork. "*That* guy

wants to see you again and you think it's not a big deal?"

Zerleena took a drink of the juice. The glass was cold and wet in her palm. Or maybe her palms were sweating. "I was hoping if I ignored him, he'd go away."

Erika inclined her head toward the newspaper in Keysha's purse. "I'd say he got closer. A lot closer." She smiled at her own joke.

Keysha shook her fork. "So what happened? Spill."

Zerleena was quiet as she sliced into her fish bake. She was still processing their conversation. It had blown her mind. And unsettled her. And left her horny. "He proposed."

"He did *what*?" Keysha's jaw dropped.

Erika was struck by a coughing fit. Zerleena kept watch over her in case she needed the Heimlich.

After seconds that felt like minutes, Erika collected herself. "He *proposed*? *Marriage*?"

"Yes." Zerleena turned back to her meal.

"He's mad." Erika drank her tea.

"Sounds like it." Keysha gave Zerleena an incredulous look. "How did he propose? I mean, he took you to an expensive restaurant. I've been to it, so I know it's the perfect place for a proposal, but did he apologize for breaking up with you? Did he explain why he'd never contacted you? Did he build up to it?"

The attorney's questioning was fast and furious. Zerleena didn't know where to start.

Erika kissed her teeth. "Last night was the first time he's seen her in more than a decade and it was the night he chose to propose. How much building up could he have done?"

"That's my point exactly. He has a lot to answer for." Keysha waved her fork in Erika's direction before returning her attention to Zerleena. "So what did he say? 'I'm in Brooklyn. You're in Brooklyn. Let's get married.'?"

Erika barked a laugh. "He's had fifteen years to prepare. I hope he did better than that." She took her time spreading butter over a slice of hardo bread.

Zerleena continued eating until her friends gave her a chance to respond. To her surprise, she felt a bit defensive on Marlon's behalf. It was ridiculous of him to expect she'd be open to his marriage proposal after his years of silence. Thinking about it made her feel like she could breathe fire. But she didn't want anyone else mocking him because of it.

Why should I care?

"So?" Keysha spread her hands. One held her fork and the other her knife. "How did he deliver this proposal, fifteen years in the making?"

Zerleena's eyes swept from Erika seated across from her to Keysha beside her. "It was pretty much what you described. He said we'd been good together in college. 'Let's get married.'"

Erika lifted her eyebrows. "He's mad."

"Wow." Keysha exhaled. "How did he explain his ignoring you for all these years?"

"He didn't." Zerleena shook her head. "He seemed to think we could just pick up where he'd left off."

Erika set down her mug. "That's why he thought he could kiss you on the first date."

Zerleena sighed, accepting a truth she hadn't wanted to face. "The thing is, if he'd proposed fifteen years ago, I would've said yes."

Erika held Zerleena's gaze. "Are the years he was away the only reason you rejected him?"

Zerleena's gaze bounced between her friends. "Isn't that enough? His *only* reason for breaking up with me was to pursue his NBA dream. Well, I had dreams, too." And they all included him.

Erika continued. "So what're you going to do now that he's here?"

Zerleena fisted her hands beneath the table. "I'm going to avoid him like my life depends on it."

Because my heart absolutely does.

***

"You've always been impulsive, Marl, but even for you, *that* was a bridge too far." Steven Crennell, Marlon's friend and former Miami Waves teammate shook his head. The former NBA superstar was now a partner with Parker Crennell Advertising. "What were you thinking, man?"

Marlon took a deep drink from his glass of ice water late Sunday morning. With Steven still in Miami, they'd agreed to stay in touch via videoconferences. Right now, Marlon wished they were texting instead. Then he could ignore the questions he didn't have answers for. The chastisement may be well-deserved. That didn't mean he wanted to hear it.

Instead he sat at his dining room table, frowning at his laptop monitor. "I was thinking the Monarchs have signed me to a one-year contract. What am I supposed to do if I have to retire at the end of the season? Leena's the only woman I've ever loved. If Father Time's trying to tell me to settle down and raise a family, there's no one else I'd even consider."

"You probably should've led with that, player." His friend was focused only on the negatives.

Steven sat in a room he insisted was his home office. Marlon had been in that room plenty of times. He knew a man cave when he saw one. The entertainment system, complete with a high-def, sixty-inch flat screen television and stereo surround sound was the first clue. Waves memorabilia and fan gear were splashed all over the pale green walls and stacked on the onyx book case. Off camera, a loveseat backed up against the fake mahogany desk where Steven sat.

Marlon grunted. "It wouldn't have helped. Leena's definitely holding a grudge over our breakup."

But how much of a grudge?

Judging by that stiff arm, a pretty sizable one.

His arms were impatient to hold her again after all these years. His groin tightened with his need to feel her melt against him and have her lips part beneath his.

"Can you blame her?" Steven's rhetorical question acted like a cold shower. "You haven't spoken with her in fifteen years. Don't get me wrong. Some people would've welcomed your silence—"

"Funny."

"She obviously didn't. But, Marl, if this is about your career, you should be talking with your agent not pissing off your college sweetheart."

Marlon leaned his head back against his cushioned dining chair, rolling it between his shoulders. It didn't do much to ease his tension. "I've talked with Jett. He's putting out feelers for teams that would be interested in picking up my contract. It's been two months and we still haven't gotten any responses."

Jett Tilden had been Marlon's agent and business manager since the start of Marlon's career. He was a former NBA player, but unlike Marlon, he'd had a plan for his retirement. He'd gone to law school. Now he used his experience as a professional athlete and his legal expertise to negotiate his clients' contracts.

"Be patient, Marl. The season's just starting." There was empathy in Steven's voice and compassion in his eyes.

Steven understood what he was going through as well as anyone could. A devastating injury had abruptly ended his friend's NBA career. Marlon had tried to support Steven during his transition from the court. Steven had been disappointed to be forced out of basketball, but he'd had a plan for life after the NBA.

Together, Marlon and Steven had founded the Nia Neighborhood Recreational Center. Its purpose — its nia — was to prepare kids — boys and girls — for success in life, with or without sports. Steven had also developed a successful career as an account executive with a well-respected, family-owned advertising firm. His talent and dedication had led to his becoming a partner with the company. Along the way, he and the daughter of the founding partner had fallen in love and married.

Marlon drained his glass of ice water. "You're right, but the farther we get into the season, the more anxious I become."

"Jett's a good agent and he's working hard for you."

"I know."

"How's it going with Marc?" Steven gave him a half smile. "Have you gotten used to his being your coach?"

"You should ask if he's gotten used to my being one of his players." Marlon's laughter joined Steven's. "We're cool. I've been going easy on him."

"I'm sure he appreciates that." Steven spread his arms in front of his desk. "Maybe you need a distraction while you wait for news from Jett."

Marlon snorted. "I'm pretty sure Leena's not going to want to see me anymore."

Steven winced. "Marl, if you're serious about reconciling with Leena, you can't treat her like a distraction."

But she was distracting him. He'd been distracted since he'd seen her last night.

Zerleena had been so familiar, and yet there was

something new about the way she'd made him feel. There was a maturity in the way she stood her ground, an assertiveness in her response. The young woman who'd been so devoted to him was gone. In her place was a woman more aware of her worth and abilities.

"How am I supposed to fix this?" Marlon scrubbed his face with both palms.

"How should I know?" Steven looked as baffled as Marlon felt.

"Of the two of us, which one is happily married?"

"I am." Steven raised his right hand. A smile eased the chiseled lines of his sienna features. "But my circumstances with Val were different from your history with Leena."

Marlon sighed. "You must have some suggestions. What do you do when Val's angry with you?"

Steven smiled, shaking his head. "If Val's in the wrong, I wait for her to come to her senses. She's stubborn, so it may take a while. If I've made a mistake, I'll apologize. It's pretty clear you're the one who messed up, player."

"I know. I know." Marlon rubbed his eyes. Frustration was popping out of his pours. "But after all this time, will an apology be enough?"

Steven grunted. "No, but it's a start."

Marlon set his glass on the jade coaster beside his laptop. "Any final tips?"

"Make sure your apology is good."

"How?" Marlon's mind went blank. He could count on both hands the number of times he'd apologized in his thirty-seven years on earth. All of those times, an 'I'm sorry' had sufficed.

Steven rolled his eyes. "Be clear. Let her know *you* know what you're apologizing for and why it was a stupid thing to do. Above all, be sincere. And good luck. It sounds like you'll need it."

They logged off after a few more minutes. He missed his friend, but these video conferences helped shrink the distance. And although he didn't have any idea how he was going to mend his relationship with Zerleena, he did feel better after talking with Steven face-to-face. Marlon carried his glass to the sink.

An apology. Zerleena deserved one, but would she accept it from him? Steven thought it was worth a try and Marlon respected his opinion. Steven and his wife, Valerie, were the happiest married couple he knew — besides his parents.

Make it a good one. Steven's counsel came back to him.

Marlon sighed. He'd better start practicing.

Chapter 3

"How could you not tell *me* that you know Marlon Burress?"

Zerleena looked up as her production intern, Dionne "D.C." Carter, strutted into their office at five A.M. Monday. As usual, the sophomore from Kings County College of Arts & Engineering was impressively put together despite the early hour. She'd accessorized her lightweight corral blue scoop neck sweater and black tapered slacks with a sapphire teardrop necklace and matching earrings. Her black suede ankle boots added four inches to her five-foot-eight-inch height as she sauntered farther into the office.

The nineteen-year-old stopped in front of Zerleena's desk and shoved her Smart phone toward her. On the screen was the *New York Horn* photo of Marlon attempting to embrace her. Each time she saw the image, Zerleena felt a vicious surge of satisfaction and a sharp, sweet pang of longing.

"I've seen the photo, but it was the print version." The online image was even clearer.

Zerleena hoped this would be her final *You-Had-Dinner-With-Marlon-Burress-And-Didn't-Tell-Me???*

inquisition. The exchanges were unraveling her nerves.

"Why didn't you tell me you were going to have dinner with *Marlon Burress*?"

"I've had other things on my mind, D.C." Zerleena cringed inside. That excuse was as lame today as it had been yesterday with Keysha and Erika.

Worse, D.C. wasn't buying it. "*You*. The *galaxy's* biggest Monarchs fan—"

"I wouldn't say that—"

"*You* had other things on your mind besides the Monarchs newest player?" D.C. crossed her arms over her chest. "I am *not* buying it."

"Why not?" It was a struggle, but Zerleena kept her eyes from wavering under D.C.'s dark, intense, brown gaze.

"I'm kind of *hurt* that you didn't *tell* me." D.C. pocketed her cell and rested her hands on the back of the gray visitor's seat in front of Zerleena's desk.

Zerleena's eyes widened. "I'm sorry. I never meant to hurt your feelings."

"When the Monarchs drafted Jamal Ward last season, you complained about it – *bitterly* - from the nanosecond they added him to the roster right up until Brooklyn hosted the champions parade for the team."

"Ward is a ball hog—"

"And I listened to *every* word, *every* syllable. I never *once* told you, you sounded insane even though you kind of did."

Zerleena's eyebrows took flight. "I did?"

"Yes, but I *never* told you."

"You told me just now." Zerleena sighed. "All right. I'm sorry I didn't tell you I know Marlon."

"*How* do you know him?"

Zerleena paused. She didn't want to remember the years she'd thought she'd been in love with him — and believed he'd loved her. "We met in college. We lost touch after he graduated." *And dumped me and started a new life in a new city. The end.*

"It must have been *more* than that for him to ask you out on a *date*. Spill." D.C. settled onto the guest chair as though she anticipated a one-woman Broadway show.

Zerleena glanced at her silver Apple iWatch. It was just after five AM. Their satellite radio show was scheduled to air in less than two hours and they still had a lot of prep work. "As much as I'd love to satisfy your prurient curiosity, we need to prepare for the show."

"Okay. I can wait." Undeterred, D.C. stood and crossed to her desk. "*But* you know I'm not the only one who's gonna want the scoop, right? A lot of your callers are going to ask about you and Marvelous Marlon as well. He's hot. You think *my* interest is prurient? I hope you're ready for *theirs. Especially* after that photo. Uh-huh, uh-huh."

Zerleena frowned. D.C. was right. "Our program's focused on women's empowerment, specifically financial freedom. I don't want the show to be distracted by meaningless gossip."

"*You're* the one who's always saying women's empowerment doesn't mean you have to live a cloistered life." D.C. turned on her laptop, then swiveled her chair to face Zerleena. Her smile was smug. "Why can't your audience see *you* walking your talk, balancing your power with an *actual* social life? How 'bout that?"

"I have a social life." It bothered her to sound so defensive. "This isn't the first time my picture's been in the paper because of some event."

D.C. shook her head. Her long braids shimmied behind her narrow shoulders. "I mean a social life that's *separate* and *apart* from building your brand."

Did D.C. have a point? At this moment, outside of her dinner with Marlon, Zerleena couldn't think of any strictly social events she'd attended. But did she want to use her dinner with Marlon as an example of her social life?

No.

"Marlon Burress isn't any part of my life, social or otherwise."

D.C. narrowed her eyes. A twinkle of mischief gleamed in their depths. "That was a pretty strong denial, considering there's *photographic evidence* to the contrary. What *exactly* was the nature of your past relationship?"

Zerleena avoided the sophomore intern's intent gaze. "Let's get to work."

D.C. abruptly straightened on her chair as though someone had pinched her. Her eyes widened with excitement. Then she looked away. "Never mind."

Not this again. "D.C., we've talked about this. A lot. I chose you for this internship out of hundreds of other applicants — mostly juniors and seniors — because your creativity will not only help me. It can launch your own career. So stop filtering. Even if I disagree with your idea, that doesn't mean it's wrong. It just isn't right for me."

The glow returned to D.C.'s round, brown features. "Okay. Well, dating Marlon Burress might be just what you need to *prove* that Cornell's *lying* when he calls you a man hater."

Ice spread over Zerleena's skin. Cornell Redd claimed to be a personal finance manager and a satellite radio show host like Zerleena. He also considered himself her competition. He wasn't. The corny troll may have a program on satellite radio, but from what Zerleena had heard on his show to date, he was *not* a personal finance manager. He was a shock jock in that it was shocking how little time he spent on personal finance.

For the past almost six months, in a transparent effort to win over Zerleena's readers and listeners, Cornell had been attacking her, claiming she hated men. She ignored him, instead choosing to focus on serving and growing her audience. For that, Cornell should be grateful. If she ever did take the fight to him, she had way more material and far more damaging subjects.

"Not to toot my own horn, but I have several best-selling books on finance and savings. I have a top-rated, award-winning satellite radio program, and speaking engagements that take me all over the country. Why would I need to acknowledge Corny's lies in any way, but especially by faking a relationship with Marlon?"

A corner of D.C.'s lips curved in a reluctant smile. "Cornell may be corny, but he's going on the air, telling people the only way your advice works is if they do what *you're* doing: sacrificing a family and a social life, and focusing only on work."

The lie stung every time she heard it. "According to our listener surveys, the majority of our audience is over thirty and married with children."

"Most people *probably* haven't seen our poll results, Leena, but Cornell's making sure everyone hears his lies." D.C.'s voice was hesitant with the insecurity of youth. Zerleena remembered that feeling well. "I don't think it's a good idea to let him *continue* to get away with this."

Her intern's concerns were valid, but she wanted to be a good role model for the budding career woman.

"I won't play his game. There's a reason more people listen to my program and that my workshops are better attended than his. I'm winning on substance. My advice is easy to follow – and it works."

D.C. spread her arms. "But if Cornell continues to spread his *lies* and you don't do *anything*, people are going to start to wonder if he's onto something."

"If a few people wander away, that's their right." Zerleena didn't feel as confident as she hoped she sounded. "When they realize his financial plans only serve his self-interests, they'll come back."

"Or they'll find someone else." A shadow of unease swept across D.C.'s round face. "Can you take that risk?"

No, but was countering Cornell's lies worth the risk of opening her heart to Marlon again? The odds of another heart break were high, probably greater than the Monarchs repeating their championship run.

***

"Don't get cocky. Pre-season game wins don't mean anything." Brooklyn Monarchs Head Coach DeMarcus Guinn addressed his team. The players were sprawled on the bleachers in the practice court during a brief break in their workout. "Last season, we lost every pre-season game, then won the championship. This year, we won every game. No one's impressed."

In his black warm-up pants and gray T-shirt, the former shooting guard looked ready to come out of retirement. During his playing days, the press had dubbed him The Mighty Guinn. Marlon knew using that nickname was the fastest way to get on DeMarcus's bad side. That's why he used it every chance he got, but never in public.

DeMarcus had earned his three NBA championships and two Most Valuable Player awards while he and Marlon had been teammates on the Miami Waves. After retirement, the future Hall of Famer and native New Yorker had returned home and took the Monarchs head coaching job. He'd used his hoops mojo to drag the league's basement-dwelling Monarchs through a miraculous Cinderella season capped by their first championship in franchise history.

Now the borough was buzzing with the will-they-or-won't-they-repeat suspense of the new season. Can the Monarchs replicate their championship run and earn their first back-to-back titles in franchise history? Marlon hoped so. He didn't want to end his successful NBA career as a loser.

He didn't want to spend his last season riding the bench, either.

Come to think of it, he didn't want to end his career.

"Speaking of cocky." Jamal "Jam-On-It" Ward, one of the team's shooting guards, jabbed his thumb over his shoulder toward Marlon. "Why'd you bring *him* onto the team?"

This wasn't the first time Jamal had asked some variation of the question. If Marlon had any regard for Jamal, the kid's attitude would have bothered him. But how could he respect someone who referred to himself in the third person — and with one of the dumbest nicknames in sports?

Jam-On-It.

Really?

Jamal had been drafted to the Monarchs last season after his first year of college. "One and done" was the technical term. His immaturity wasn't surprising, but Marlon would bet two of his two championship rings the kid had given himself that goofy moniker.

A muscle flexed in DeMarcus's jaw. Not a good sign. "Asked and answered, Jamal. Stop wasting our time."

That Jamal didn't heed DeMarcus's warning was further evidence of the kid's galactic lack of wisdom. "I know what you *didn't* tell us. You *didn't* tell us that you brought him here because he's your friend and the Waves don't want him anymore."

Outwardly, Marlon didn't react to the taunt. Not so much as a muscle twitched. But ice shifted in his gut. There was truth in that statement, but how much? Had DeMarcus convinced his fiancée and franchise owner, Jaclyn Jones, to pick up Marlon's contract? And had she agreed to his request but for only one season?

DeMarcus's almond-shaped coal black eyes cooled on Jamal. Standing beside him in front of the bleachers, Oscar Clemente, the Monarchs assistant head coach, dragged his chubby tan fingers through what was left of his graying hair.

The older man shook his head as though, even after a full season of Jamal's crap, he couldn't believe the young shooting guard's recklessness. "You keep pissing off the wrong people, and you're going to end you're career."

DeMarcus took a step toward the bleachers where Jamal sprawled with overconfidence. His cold stare kept Jamal pinned in place. Whatever his friend was going to say would undoubtedly crush the younger man's ego. But this wasn't DeMarcus's battle. The taunt hadn't been meant for his friend. It had been intended for him.

Marlon turned toward his young teammate and affected his trademark taunting smile. It was a bit amused and a little mean. He'd seen it rattle even his toughest rivals. Jamal looked like he was going to faint.

Marlon interrupted before DeMarcus could speak. "Miami wanted younger players, but they didn't ask for you. Instead they asked for the Monarchs *future* picks. They'd rather wait for an unknown than add you to their roster. That must sting."

Jamal's brown skin flushed to his clean-shaven head. He sprang from the bleachers, fists clenched. "That's bullshit, old man."

It was cold comfort that Marlon was better adept at controlling his reaction to the taunts of other players. But then, he'd had more practice. "Don't dish it if you can't take it, rook."

Jamal's nostrils flared. "I'm not a rookie anymore, but you're even older."

"Sit down, Jamal." Warrick Evans, the Monarchs' star shooting guard and reigning league MVP, sounded weary. There was tension on his copper features. His brown eyes were irritated as though he'd seen this particular movie before and liked it even less the second time around.

Jamal hesitated before following Warrick's orders.

That the hotheaded player had listened to the veteran impressed Marlon. It showed him who held the most influence over the team, and it wasn't Barron "Bling" Douglas, the point guard and team captain who was returning after ending the season on the Injured List. Like the rest of the Monarchs, Barron had remained quiet during the exchange between DeMarcus, Marlon, and Jamal "Goofy" Ward.

Marlon considered the players. The starters: Warrick, Jamal, forward Serge Gateau, center Vincent Jardine, and forward Anthony "St. Anthony" Chambers.

Point guard Darius Williams and shooting guard Roger Harris had seen a lot of playing time during the playoffs. Although they were seated near him, Marlon sensed they were far away. Did they share Jamal's suspicions of why he was here? Was that the reason he felt blocked out?

Or were they still angry about the Waves versus Monarchs conference finals? The competition hadn't been filled with chocolates, hearts, and flowers. In the end, the Monarchs had beaten the Waves. Marlon wasn't holding a grudge so why were they?

DeMarcus brought their focus back to their practice session. "As I said, don't get confident with our pre-season standing. Those other teams were toying with us."

"I agree." Marlon's response was reflexive. He hadn't intended to share his thoughts.

Jamal leaped at his words anyway. "You're not the coach. Ain't nobody care what you think."

Marlon cocked his head. "Do I intimidate you, rook?"

Jamal's nostrils flared. "I told you I'm not a rook."

Marlon ignored the anger stirring in his gut and curled his lips in mockery. "You think just because you have one season under your belt, you're not a rookie anymore, rook?"

DeMarcus lowered his clipboard. He split his glare between Marlon and Jamal. "I'm not putting up with this for an entire season. It ends now."

The admonishment made Marlon feel like a child. He wouldn't be surprised to learn that had been DeMarcus's point. Even as an NBA player, DeMarcus had earned a reputation as a hard taskmaster. It was as though basketball was a game to everyone but him.

Marlon drew deep, even breaths, trying to relax. The scent of honest sweat battled with the lemon wax that made the hardwood practice court gleam.

But Jamal once again ignored DeMarcus's warning. "Why did we trade draft picks for this also-ran has-been? He's not taking my spot."

Marlon had suspected the narcissistic point guard's fear of being benched was behind his anger. But DeMarcus had already announced the starting roster. To Marlon's disappointment, his friend of almost two decades was keeping the lineup from last season's championship run: Warrick, Vincent, Anthony, Serge, and Jamal. Marlon was coming off the bench. Despite DeMarcus's decision, Jamal remained insecure.

Anthony appeared to have doubts as well. "Our first game's Wednesday at the Spurs. That's only two days from now. Shouldn't we know whether the starting lineup is final so we can prepare?"

"If you know the playbook, you'll be prepared." DeMarcus arched a thick eyebrow. "And for the last time, the starters *are* final. Keep your insecurities off my court. I'm not your therapist."

Jamal glowered. "Your boy ain't taking my spot, Coach."

DeMarcus's features were stiff with anger. "Same rules as last season, Jamal. You've got to earn your spot every night." He turned to the rest of the team. "Practice's over."

Marlon stood with relief and followed the Monarchs to the locker room.

Like Jamal, Marlon didn't want to be a bench warmer. But he couldn't see his friend-now-coach breaking up a championship roster to accommodate him.

Between warming the bench and Jamal's hostility, this was going to be a long season. Retirement seemed inevitable. But who was he without basketball?

Chapter 4

"Imagine running into you here." A familiar yet dreaded singsong voice carried over Zerleena's shoulder.

Bracing herself, she turned to face her former college classmate in the business section of her favorite independent bookstore. "Carol."

Carol Mart had been one of the five people with whom Zerleena had rented an apartment during her junior and senior years. Moving in together had seemed like a good idea at first.

The other woman's bright smile didn't reach her powder blue eyes. "I was just across the street in the diner over there when I saw you come into the store. At least, I thought it was you. Every time I see you, I'm just amazed! You haven't changed since college. You look exactly the same. What's your secret?"

Zerleena assessed the other woman's milky complexion, honey blond hair, and calculating eyes. Her words weren't meant as a compliment. Zerleena knew her well enough to recognize the dig. Her former housemate had hoped to trigger Zerleena's past insecurities by reminding her of the awkward college student she'd been. She probably hoped doing so would give her the upper hand in whatever she was planning.

Unfortunately for Carol, those youthful memories didn't make her as uncomfortable as they used to. On her rigid student budget, She'd watched every dime, focusing on necessities, cutting coupons, and stocking her wardrobe with purchases from second-hand stores. Those actions had helped her manage her tight budget.

In contrast, Carol seemed to still have an unrestrained desire for expensive fashion, judging by the tailored powder blue pantsuit that matched her eyes and hugged her full figure. Her designer navy blue stilettos, which added at least four inches to her five-foot-nine-inch height, could be knockoffs. However, her rose-gold watch and the dangling three-quarter cut diamond-and-yellow-gold earrings were not.

"You were right. It's me." Zerleena dredged up a smile. Marlon Saturday night; Carol this afternoon. It was her college reunion nightmare.

"What are the odds you and I would be in the same place at the same time?" Carol settled her hands on her hips. "And then on Sunday, I saw that photo of you and Marlon Burress on social media."

Zerleena had hoped her polite smile would discourage this discussion. It hadn't.

"Are you and Marlon getting back together?" Carol's eyes searched Zerleena's expression. Was she looking for hints about her personal life?

"It was nice to catch up with you." Zerleena continued down the aisle, skimming book titles.

Carol followed. "You two were pretty hot and heavy

in college. You know, we all just assumed you'd be to-gether after graduation. It's a good thing we didn't put any money on it. Right? We'd have gone broke." She laughed at her joke.

With her back to the other woman, Zerleena made herself relax. "I suppose so."

"Some of us thought Marlon didn't want to be tied down, you know, when he started his basketball ca-reer."

She'd had enough. "If you'll excuse me, I have to leave for—"

"*You're* looking at finance books?" Carol's attention had moved to the books visible over Zerleena's shoul-der. She let out a trilling laugh. "*You?* I thought you knew everything there was to know about the subject. After all, you're *Zerleena Chase* of *Zerleena's She Shed*. You've written money management books yourself."

Zerleena lost patience with Carol's transparent at-tempts to push all of her buttons. She decided to try a few of her own. "What about you, Carol? Are you still throwing parties?"

Carol's eyes cooled under the direct hit. "I'm an *event planner*. I don't *throw parties*. I plan. Events."

Zerleena pretended to check her wristwatch. "Yes, well, I should—"

"Aren't you hosting an event next month, one of your workshops?" Carol's pleasant tone triggered Zer-leena's internal warning system.

"My next workshop is in mid-November."

"That's right. Next month. Right before the holidays. Isn't that an inconvenient time? You're going to conflict with all the shopping."

"My goal is to encourage people to think about their budget and do a financial checkup *before* they get carried away with their holiday shopping."

"Oh, I see." Carol trilled another laugh. "I've been so surprised by all the good things I've heard about your workshops."

"Thank you." *I think.*

Carol shrugged. "I don't suppose you have a friends-and-family discount." Another laugh.

Even if she did, Carol wouldn't qualify for either. Still, these conversations were awkward. She'd learned the hard way she had to draw a line between being a businesswoman and being a friend. Without that line, people weren't taking her seriously. Friends would want "special pricing" for themselves. Then they'd want discounts for their friends. It had gotten out of control. But Zerleena had learned the importance of promoting the value of the information. Most of her friends understood her decision. Others ... well, perhaps they'd never been friends.

Zerleena spread her hands. "No, I don't. But if you aren't able to attend the November workshop, the information we're reviewing is in my books."

"Well, I'm sorry to tell you this, Leena, but your books aren't easy to read." Carol's tone was vindictive.

"I'm sorry you find the books challenging." But not surprised.

In college, Carol had put the minimum effort into

her studies. Still, the other woman's feedback provided food for thought. She made a mental note to consider ways to make the concepts in her money management basics book even easier to understand.

"They're not challenging." Carol was terse. "They're hard to understand. That's why I wanted to go to the workshop. I thought hearing you talk about it would help me."

Zerleena considered the diamond earrings, matching necklace, and rose-gold watch that accessorized Carol's tailored pantsuit. Her workshop cost a fraction of what the other woman had spent on her outfit. It wasn't that Carol *couldn't* understand how to get her finances in order. She wasn't ready to.

"My registration's in line with similar workshops on my topic." Zerleena maneuvered around Carol, intent on making her way to the checkout counter.

"Well, I'm sorry you can't see your way to helping out a friend, Leena." Carol shifted, tracking Zerleena's escape. "I hope *you* don't find yourself needing a favor in the near future."

"Take care, Carol."

The other woman grunted.

She heard Carol's anger and spite. She was sorry the other woman was upset, but she couldn't allow personal feelings to make her second guess her decisions. She was already doing too much of that with Marlon back in her life.

***

The practice court was empty. The other players — his new teammates — had long since left him behind. Only the scent of sweat and lemon floor wax had waited for him. Marlon hadn't expected anything else.

He adjusted his green sport bag on his shoulder as he crossed the court. His sneakers squeaked against the hardwood floor. The Brooklyn Monarchs' black-and-silver crown logo mocked him from center court. He was in their house now, and their house was supposed to be his.

Then why did he feel as though he was in their doghouse?

Getting used to a new team in a new city was no joke. He'd played his entire professional career in Miami. He'd built his life there. His parents had moved there. He'd left all of that behind when he'd moved to Brooklyn. Here, the only people he knew were a former teammate who was now his boss and an ex-girlfriend who wanted him to lose her number.

Marlon climbed a winding stairwell that led to a wide tan hallway. He continued toward the building's exit and the stench of burned popcorn. Who kept burning the shit? There was a button on the microwave marked Popcorn. Just push it. If these geniuses couldn't figure that out, how were they going to make the playoffs much less win the title?

His sneakers continued squeaking down the hall. The Monarchs logo was emblazoned on the wall to his right. Natural light flowed through the glass front façade, flooding the space.

Several trainers and teammates occupied the lounge area on the left. A few played pool at one of the tables. Another pair used the Ping-Pong table. A group sprawled on the comfortable sofas and stylish armchairs that featured the franchise logo and team colors while they watched a sporting event on the large, high-def television mounted from the ceiling. They were snacking on some of the healthy selections from the nearby vending machines. Marlon again wondered which one of those bozos had burned the popcorn.

In the conversation area on the other side of the machines, DeMarcus sat with Warrick and the Monarchs vice president of marketing, Troy Marshall. The six-two former college hoops star looked like he could still play some ball. With his glossy black curls, and perfectly shaped mustache and goatee, he also looked like he could star in daytime television dramas.

Marlon felt more comfortable approaching them since DeMarcus was there. He knew he had to conquer his unease with the other members of his new team, but that was a lot of negativity to get through. He was having trouble finding the time and energy for it.

Troy arched a thick black eyebrow as he pointed toward Marlon. "Do you need help finding Monarchs gear?"

Marlon looked down at his green and blue Waves jersey. "Sorry, man. I wasn't thinking."

"That's not going to earn you any points in the locker room." DeMarcus's advice was subtle but effective.

Marlon glanced at Warrick before returning his attention to his coach. "Point taken."

"How long have you known Zerleena Chase?" Troy changed the subject.

"How'd you know we knew each other?" Was the executive clairvoyant? Could he tell whether he'd earn another championship ring this season?

DeMarcus grinned at Marlon's amazement. "You may want to take a look at the *Horn*'s Sunday social section. There's a photo of the two of you outside of that restaurant I told you about."

Warrick called up the photo on his Smart phone. "Here."

Marlon took the device from the shooting guard. His eyes widened at the image of the two of them.

Damn, how could she be even more beautiful now?

He dragged his attention from her features to read the caption beneath the photo. He smiled at the reference to her stiff-arming him.

"Financial wizard?" Marlon returned Warrick's phone.

"We've known each other for fifteen years." DeMarcus's eyebrows knitted. "You've never mentioned her."

Marlon shrugged, pretending he'd known Zerleena was a local celebrity. Were those stares at the restaurant meant for her? "Yeah, well a guy wants some privacy even from good friends."

DeMarcus laughed. "Considering your favorite topic of conversation is you, I find that hard to believe. How do you know her?"

"Leena and I dated in college." Marlon shoved his hands into the front pockets of his navy blue cargo shorts. His head spun as he tried to reconcile the unassuming young woman he'd loved in college with the empire builder he wanted to get to know better.

"Jack's been listening to her radio show for years. She told Andrea and Mary about it." DeMarcus gestured toward Warrick and Troy. "We've all read most if not all of her books and listen to her show."

Dr. Marilyn DeVry-Evans was an obstetrician-gynecologist and Warrick's wife. And according to team gossip, Troy had been dating *The New York Times* reporter Andrea Benson since last season.

"That's ... amazing." Marlon couldn't think of any other way to express his wonder. He was overwhelmed. He'd known she was successful — very successful. And she used her wealth to support community causes anonymously. But he hadn't realized she was famous.

Instead he'd been focused on himself, his career, his retirement, and how this team trade had changed his life. What else was he ignorant of regarding Zerleena?

***

"Did anyone else catch the photo of Zerleena

Chase with Brooklyn's newest Monarch, Marlon Burress?" Cornell Redd's tone was smug as he opened his Monday evening satellite radio program, Reddy to Earn.

Zerleena tensed as she waited for the broadcaster to lob the obvious insult his question had set up.

Why do I torture myself listening to his show?

She was taking a dinner break from her next money management for novices manuscript. She'd gone back into the draft document file and made some notes based on her earlier encounter with Carol.

Zerleena settled at her kitchen table with her roasted chicken and garden salad. Her bright and cheery room, decorated in pale pastels against a blonde wood background didn't seem like such a happy space right now.

Cornell viewed himself as Zerleena's competitor. He'd missed the part about a competitor needing to compete. Her book sales eclipsed his. Her radio audience outnumbered his. Her money management workshops were better attended. Based on the numbers, Zerleena was competing against herself.

But to keep up with her industry, it was important to know what other advisers — even the lame ones — were saying.

"Why would a guy like Marlon Burress — an elite athlete, two-time NBA champion, and future Hall of Famer — waste his time wining and dining a man hater like Zerleena Chase? She'd even blocked the guy when he was going for a good-night kiss." Cornell continued his unwarranted attack.

Zerleena glared at her silver-and-black cell phone. She was using the device to listen to Cornell's program. "Are you going to spend your entire two-hour program on this?" Unable to hear her, Cornell didn't respond.

"I mean, did he lose a bet?" Cornell laughed at what he must have considered a joke. "Tell me what you think, listeners."

Zerleena hesitated with her right index finger over her cell phone's touchscreen. Her background image was the Monarchs logo. How would Cornell's listeners react to his lead-in topic? Was this the kind of content they wanted?

His show hadn't always been this way. He'd devolved into this format a couple of weeks ago in a lame attempt to discredit her. Zerleena drank her iced tea and started on her salad. She may be in need of the fortification.

"Our first caller. Who's on the line?" Cornell asked.

"Scott from Queens." A grumpy voice responded.

Zerleena's muscles bunched as she waited for the caller's verdict.

"Thanks for calling, Scott from Queens." Cornell was upbeat and amused. "Tell us what you think about Marlon Burress going out with Zerleena."

"Why are we talking about this?" Scott went on the attack. "I thought this was a show for financial advice. If I want to talk about which celebrities are dating each other ... Well, I don't. Ever."

She almost choked on a cucumber slice. *Now* that *was funny.*

"Thanks for your feedback, Scott." Cornell wasn't as jovial now. "Just for your information Scott and anyone else who missed the message, in addition to giving money advice, I consider myself a life coach, like Zerleena."

She raised her eyebrows and stared at her cell. "I don't know whose life you're coaching, Corny, but they might want to ask for a trade to another team."

Cornell's comparison continued. "But unlike me, Zerleena shouldn't be giving *anyone* relationship advice. Next caller."

"And you shouldn't be giving anyone any advice." Zerleena's finger hovered over her touchscreen again. She stopped when the next caller introduced herself.

"This is D.C. from Brooklyn," The young female voice said.

D.C. from Brooklyn? Oh, no! Zerleena lost her breath. Blood rushed out of her head. Why was her production intern calling into Corny's show?

"Go ahead, D.C. from Brooklyn. What do you think about Marlon and Zerleena getting together?" Cornell's good cheer sounded forced.

Zerleena held her head in her hands as she waited for D.C.'s response.

"I agree with your *first* caller." D.C. sounded as though she was daring the radio show host to disagree with the listeners. "*Why* are you talking about Zerleena Chase's love life when you're *supposed* to be giving people financial advice? Is it because you know she's more *knowledgeable* than you about *everything* to do with financial matters?"

"That's your opinion, and your opinion's wrong." Cornell was barely maintaining his mockery. "Zerleena may know some things about investing, but she definitely needs help with her love life."

I *need help with my love life*? She gave her cell the side eye. "People who live in glasshouses shouldn't throw stones, Corny."

D.C.'s uproarious laughter interrupted the radio host. "Leena Chase doesn't need dating advice from someone who hasn't had a date since senior prom."

Zerleena hastily swallowed her iced tea. That was mean. Funny, but mean. Should she text her intern, telling her to end the call?

"Wrong again." Cornell's amusement disappeared. "If you kept up with my media coverage, you'd know that I date. A lot. Zerleena could benefit from my success in the dating arena. If she came on my show, I could give her some tips."

D.C. snorted. "Zerleena's never coming on your show. Why should she help your ratings?"

Zerleena could picture her friend rolling her eyes. "Good job, D.C. Thank you. Now hang up."

"You know, D.C. You have a point." Cornell's gloating was back. "Zerleena wouldn't agree to come on my show. She knows she wouldn't be able to go toe-to-toe with me."

D.C.'s gasp echoed Zerleena's. "She'd destroy—"

Cornell cut her off. "She'd be outmatched and out-classed on Reddy to Earn."

D.C. tried to talk over Cornell. "That's bull—"

Cornell again interrupted. "So instead of inviting *her*, I'm going to reach out to Marlon Burress with an invitation to Reddy to Earn. Are you listening, Mr. Burress? You can expect a call from me very shortly."

Zerleena stared blindly across her kitchen and through the sliding glass doors that led to her balcony. She should have sent the text telling D.C. to end her call with Corny. If she had, she wouldn't have needed to make this call. Zerleena checked the time on her cell phone. It was just after five P.M. Marlon should be done with the team's practice for the day. Not that she'd memorized the team's practice schedule or anything like that. Anyway ...

With a heavy sigh, she selected his number from her cell phone's list of recent calls. Her movements were slow, reluctant as she forced herself to make the call. After several rings she went into his voicemail. Her sigh of relief that she wouldn't have to speak with him yet caught in her throat. It was replaced by an aching groan as his rich, deep voice sounded in her ear. Marlon looked good. He sounded good.

But he wasn't good for you. Remember that.

Zerleena cleared her throat and waited for the sound of the beep. "It's Leena. We need to talk."

Chapter 5

"How did you get my address?" Zerleena crossed her condo building's lobby Monday evening. She didn't seem happy to see him.

"I followed you Saturday night." Marlon straightened from the wall. The exasperation in her eyes told him giving her space after their dinner hadn't helped his cause.

She gaped at him. "In New York traffic at night?"

"I didn't say it had been easy. You said we needed to talk." He'd thought her message had referred to rekindling their relationship. He'd obviously been wrong.

What else did they have to talk about besides getting back together?

Judging by her tone and the look on her face, he'd missed something.

"Yes, we need to talk. On the phone." Zerleena sighed, shaking her head. "Come on, then."

Marlon accepted her less-than-gracious invitation. She tossed a smile to the security guard at the front desk on her way to the elevators. The older gentleman returned it and added a wave.

But she had yet to smile at him or address him by name.

Marlon swallowed a sigh of regret as he joined her in the elevator. "You didn't tell me you were a celebrity."

The elevator's metal walls were polished to a mirror finish, casting their images back to them. He could look his fill at her stunning features and fit figure without her accusing him of staring at her.

Zerleena gave him a surprised smile. "If I were a celebrity, I wouldn't have to tell you." Her eyes twinkled in her heart-shaped face.

Marlon's heart punched his chest. Her smile was even more beautiful than he'd remembered. He sank into her gaze. "I'm serious, Leena." He cleared his throat. "I knew you were a regular on *The New York Times* best-sellers list and that your radio show was successful. But I didn't realize the paparazzi followed you around New York."

She rolled her eyes. "I could do without that kind of attention. Are you reconsidering your marriage proposal?"

"We had a good thing in college. I know we could be good together again."

"After college, you dumped me because I was inconvenient. What makes me more convenient now?" Zerleena slipped between the elevator doors before they'd fully opened. It was a testament to her irritation.

Marlon followed her, scrambling for a persuasive argument. "I know we haven't kept in touch—"

"That's an understatement." She tossed the words

over her shoulder as she unlocked her door. She crossed into her condo, seeming not to care whether Marlon followed her. "It's like saying, 'Winning an NBA title is a nice accomplishment' or 'Being league MVP is swell.'"

"So you *have* followed my career." Marlon felt a rush of relief. And excitement.

His grin faded and died under her scathing glare.

"What. An. Ego." She walked farther into her condo.

He followed. "You're still the same woman I fell in love with in college."

Zerleena abruptly stopped to face him. "You fell in love with me in college?"

He smiled. "Yes."

"Then why did you break up with me?"

"I ..." *Don't have an answer.*

"God, save me from egotistical men."

Marlon frowned. "What?"

"You're wrong. I'm not that gushing groupie who'd followed you around campus, singing your praises and boosting your ego. To say I am proves you no longer know me." She spread her arms. "I'm my own person now and I recognize my own worth."

She'd caught him off guard. As he'd packed up his home in Miami to relocate to Brooklyn, he'd created a mental image of himself asking Zerleena to marry him. Sure he'd have to do some persuasion, offer an apology for his years of absence. But that would only take a few minutes. By the end of their romantic dinner, he'd had her tearfully agreeing to be his wife. Never had he considered she'd flat out reject his proposal and subsequent pleas for reconsideration. Reality was a disappointment.

"You think the only reason I'm interested in you is that I want someone who idolizes me?"

"Yes." She walked farther from him. "But no one could possibly idolize you as much as you do."

Marlon closed the distance between them. "Leena, I'm not looking for a fan."

"Oh, that's right. You're looking for a uterus." She made a rude noise.

Marlon paused to take in the surroundings. He'd been curious about her home. It was spotless, a sharp contrast to his condo. He sensed a ruthless discipline that wouldn't allow anything to be left "laying around." The warm reddish mahogany flooring gleamed beneath his feet. Natural light poured in through large picture windows in the adjoining room and played off the chalk white walls. The effect made the entryway appear bright and spacious.

The arch to the left opened to Zerleena's living room. It was decorated in shades of silver and black. Marlon smiled. She was a lifelong, diehard Brooklyn Monarchs fan. The abundance of leafy green plants beside her window and the fireplace alcove painted red provided the only relief from her Monarchs fandom.

"I didn't want to talk with you about the past."

Zerleena's words brought his attention back to the woman he wanted more now than ever before.

"What did you want to talk about?"

She turned away to cross into her living room. Marlon followed.

"Cornell Redd is a money management consultant. Or he says he is." Zerleena spoke with her back to him as she faced her fireplace. From the contempt in her voice, Marlon suspected there was at least one person she held in less esteem than him. "He's trying to raise his business profile — and client base — by attacking me on his show."

Marlon felt a hot rush of anger. "What do you mean by 'attacking' you?"

She turned to face him. "It's a long story and not worth getting into. The point is he found out we know each other. He's going to invite you onto his show to dig for dirt about me. I'd consider it a personal favor if you'd decline his invitation."

Marlon's muscles trembled with temper. His legs were stiff as he stepped forward. "Leena, please talk to me. Who is this guy and what's he doing?"

Zerleena held his gaze for several silent moments before looking away. She paced the length of her living room. "He thinks he's a competitor. He plans workshops modeled after mine. And he has a satellite radio show that he promotes as a rival to my show."

"Zerleena's She Shed."

Her eyebrows rose. "That's right. Have you listened

to it?" The guarded look in her eyes conflicted with the hopeful note in her voice.

His heart squeezed. "Yes, I have. I've learned a few things from you."

"How hard would it have been to let me know that?"

"I'm sorry." It was hard to explain and something in the tense, angry lines of her body told him now wasn't the time to try. "The Monarchs franchise owner loves your show."

"Jackie Jones? Cool." Zerleena's arched eyebrows disappeared beneath her bangs. But some of the enthusiasm had faded from her gaze.

He crossed his arms. "So Redd's jealous of you."

"That's an understatement." Her tone was dry. She paced the room. "His latest plan is to convince people I hate men."

"What?"

"I know. He's such an idiot." Her voice quickened, keeping up with her strides. "He claims I'm telling women the only way they can be successful is to sacrifice personal relationships. He thinks that's what I've done so that's what I'm promoting on my show, during my workshops, and in my books. Of course, he's lying."

Marlon cocked his head, frowning. "When you asked God to save you from arrogant men — plural — were you referring to Redd *and* me?"

Zerleena angled her chin defiantly. "That's right."

She'd lumped him in with this jerk. That stung.

"Don't worry. I won't give this guy an interview." His decision was met with silence.

Zerleena narrowed her gaze. "That's it? You're going to do this favor for me?"

Marlon smiled at the suspicion glinting in her eyes. "No, I mean I'm *not* doing any favors for *him*." He turned to leave. "See you la—"

"Wait." She crossed to within an arm's length of him. In her sneakers, the top of her head came to the middle of his chest. "You don't expect anything in return?"

Marlon's eyes lifted away from hers and swept her living room again. The quiet girl with the unforgiving budget had become a successful entrepreneur with her own radio show, best-selling books, and a lit condo.

He dropped his arms and returned his gaze to hers. She had the most amazing eyes. "There's one thing."

Zerleena crossed her arms and angled a knowing look up at him. "I thought so. What is it?"

"Say my name."

Zerleena blinked. Caution entered the warm brown depths of her wide eyes. "What?"

"You haven't said my name since we've reconnected. I want to hear you say it. Please." His pulse raced in his throat.

She arched a skeptical eyebrow. "If I say your name one time, you'll reject Cornell's invitation to appear on his show?"

"That's right."

Zerleena held his eyes for a silent moment. Then she whispered. "Marlon."

Muscles flexed in his abdomen. He lowered his head to taste his name on her lips. It was a brief sample, then he raised his head. "You're right, Leena. I don't know you anymore, but I want to."

Shaking her head, Zerleena stepped back. "If this is some new mind game you're playing, just stop. We're not going back to the way we were."

"I'm not asking to go back. I want to go forward with you. Could we try being friends?" His lips curved in a reluctant smile. "I can use a friend these days."

It took a moment or two, but the doubt finally left her expression. "All right."

His heart was heavy as he rode the elevator back to the lobby. How had he allowed this to happen? While he'd been collecting accolades, awards, and championships, he'd burned all bridges to the one person who'd been there when he hadn't believed in himself. Could he ever make it up to her?

Would she let him?

***

"Yo, Monarchs! Meet my girl." Jamal's shout drew Marlon's attention.

The lanky shooting guard strutted farther into the practice facility's lounge. He adjusted the strap of his red gym bag across his chest. The woman with him clung to his left arm like an additional limb.

With practice over, Jamal had changed into his usual dark blue jeans and white T-shirt. He looked like a toddler playing dress up with his father's clothes. The pant legs sagged over his shoes and the T-shirt hung past his knees. His heavy custom-designed, gold chain spelled out Jam-On-It. The nickname rested on his abdomen.

Marlon, Warrick, Troy, and DeMarcus rose from their seats. On closer observation, the woman looked at least ten years older than their twenty-year-old teammate. Perhaps the heavy makeup accentuating her brown features coupled with her air of maturity gave that impression. The bone-straight brown tresses looked like an inexpensive weave. They swung around her full hips in the tight denim shorts. Her outfit was accessorized with chunky gold earrings and several heavy gold necklaces. She and Jamal must have the same jeweler.

"Coach. Troy. Rick. Marlon. This is my girl, Tammy." Jamal muttered the introductions before returning his attention to his cell phone.

Tammy unlatched herself from Jamal's arm and invaded Marlon's personal space. "And what do you do?" She stared at him as though she knew what he looked like naked.

Marlon held his ground, though the hunger in Tammy's eyes made him want to back away. Far, far away. He didn't need his imaginary Honey Decoder Ring to know Tammy would elicit the red light response. "I play basketball."

"Is that the only thing you play?" Tammy's tongue circled her pouty lips.

How would Jamal react to his girlfriend's blatant flirting with a teammate? A quick glance at him confirmed that his attention remained glued to his phone.

Marlon shoved Tammy's hand from his chest. "Jamal's my teammate. I don't play those games."

Tammy lowered her voice. "Your loss." She turned her attention to Warrick.

The shooting guard took a step back. "Don't look over here."

Troy shook his head. DeMarcus stared her down.

Irritation sparked in Tammy's dark brown eyes. She spun to Jamal. "These clowns don't have nuthin' on you, Jam-On-It. Let's go."

Jamal lowered his phone. A goofy grin split his face. "She's fine, right? And smart, too. Saw right away that Jam-On-It was the star on this team. You losers ain't got nuthin' over me." He cracked a laugh, then turned to lead Tammy past the security guard and through the facility's glass front doors.

Tammy threw a venomous look toward Marlon and the others over her shoulder before leading Jamal out to the parking lot.

Marlon stared after them. "That's the first time I've heard someone other than Jamal refer to him as Jam-On-It."

DeMarcus grunted. "Unless you see her again, it's also the last."

"Do you think Jamal knows his girlfriend flirts with other men?" Troy asked.

Warrick shook his head. "I can't see Jamal with a woman who isn't as obsessed with him as he is with himself."

Marlon silently agreed. "I don't think it was Jamal's idea to introduce her to the team. I think Tammy wanted to meet us."

Troy frowned. "What makes you think that?"

"If it was his idea, he'd have introduced her to all of us." Marlon jerked a thumb over his shoulder. "The rest of the team are on the other side of the wall. Instead Jamal left as soon as Tammy said she wanted to go."

DeMarcus nodded. "Good point."

Troy sent a look around the group. "So who's going to tell Jamal that Tammy's scouting his teammates?"

Marlon wasn't the only one who looked to Warrick.

"Don't look over here." The league MVP settled the strap of his gym bag onto his shoulder, then strode away. He greeted the security guard on duty by name before pushing through the doors.

"If the kid's happy, I'm happy." DeMarcus broke the brief silence. "But I hope Tammy doesn't become a distraction. We have enough of those."

Marlon had a feeling his coach's hopes were in vain. His imaginary Honey Decoder Ring was never wrong.

***

"It's good to see you, man." Marlon saluted Steven with a glass of ice water. His longtime friend had arranged this videoconference that was streaming his image onto Marlon's laptop.

Steven returned the salute with his glass. "We can't let our travel night tradition end just because we're a few hundred miles apart."

Marlon forced a laugh. "Traditions have to evolve."

Early into their playing days, Steven had realized Marlon hated to fly. Really, really hated to fly. He still did. One night before a travel day, Steven had shown up at Marlon's home with crappy popcorn and DVDs of crappier movies. They'd continued the tradition despite Steven's early retirement and marriage. Steven's kindness and generosity was the reason Marlon considered him more than a friend. He was his brother.

Valerie Parker-Crennell, Steven's bride of four years, entered the screen. She stood behind Steven's desk chair and smiled at Marlon's image on Steven's computer monitor. Her inky black hair swung forward over her slender shoulders. "It's good to see you, Marlon. Miami's not the same without you."

"Val! Steve still treating you right?" Marlon's question was unnecessary. He'd never seen a happier couple.

Valerie rested a hand on Steven's shoulder. "He makes me feel like a queen."

Steven reached up to cover her hand with his. The

couple exchanged a look that could have been a renewal of their wedding vows.

Marlon felt a twinge of envy. "As he should. You deserve it. But if he ever steps out of line, I'll be on the next flight to Miami to set him straight."

Valerie laughed like he knew she would. "Thanks, Marlon, but I can handle him."

Marlon winked. "No doubt."

Valerie pulled her gaze from her husband. "Travel safely. And good luck against the Spurs."

Marlon coaxed his muscles to relax. Between the flight, playing on a new team, and coming off of that team's bench, he had a lot to worry about.

"Thanks, Val." He returned her parting smile, then shifted his attention back to Steven once they were alone again. "I hope you know how lucky you are."

Steven nodded. "I do. She's a solid gold on the Honey Decoder Ring."

Marlon had often joked about wishing he had an actual Honey Decoder Ring, a device that provided color-coded relationship signals. In his opinion, every baller needed one.

For example, if a woman he was interested in just wanted a good time, the ring would glow green. If she was planning to set him up for a paternity suit, the ring would burn red. An amber light meant proceed with caution. If the ring glowed gold, then she was the honey for him.

"What's with all the dirty clothes? Are you in your

laundry room?" Steven's question pulled Marlon from his envy.

He frowned, looking around his living room. "I don't have a laundry room, Mister Clean Freak. And these clothes aren't dirty. I'm in the middle of packing."

"How much do you have to pack? It's just two days."

"You know I have a process, man." Marlon lifted his eyebrows, daring his friend to give him more grief.

Steven wisely changed the subject. "How's the transition going with Marc?"

Marlon didn't like this topic any better than their last. "The Mighty One gave me The Talk this morning. I have to win the locker room."

Steven expelled a heavy breath. "He's right. It stinks, but if you want to be successful on your new team, you're going to have to win your teammates' trust."

Marlon dragged a hand over his hair. The tension in his neck and shoulders expanded like a balloon. "They don't even trust each other. That's the reason they don't play like a team. And even if I win them over, I'm still coming off the bench."

"I get it. Coming off the bench when you're used to starting is hard."

"It's also a sign I'm coming to the end of my career."

"We want to come out of the game on our own terms. We don't want someone or something else making the decision for us." A shadow moved over Steven's features.

Marlon was silent for a beat. He remembered the play that had ended Steven's career. He felt the injury as though it had happened to him. Watching his friend pack up his locker for the last time had wrecked him.

"Maybe if the Monarchs don't extend my contract, my agent can arrange a trade for me to another team." Marlon waited for Steven's response.

"Maybe." His friend seemed dubious.

So was Marlon. What if no other team picked him up? Did he want the specter of ending his career as the player other teams passed over?

No, he didn't.

Steven continued. "Talk with Jackie Jones. Ask her what her plans are for you after this season. I've heard she's one of the good ones as far as team owners, and she used to be a player. She'll understand your concern."

If only it was that easy. "Marc would've told me if Jackie was considering extending my contract."

"Marc wouldn't want to be in the middle. Neither would I. And neither would you. Talk with Jackie."

"Alright, I'll do that." But what if she confirmed his fear this would be his only season with the Monarchs?

Chapter 6

"I wish you wouldn't let that windbag Cornell Redd attack your reputation." Jillian Chase voiced her familiar complaint Wednesday evening. "It's not right."

Zerleena was helping her parents clean their kitchen after their weekly family dinner. She was careful to pack the dishwasher in the manner she knew her mother preferred.

The kitchen was one of the prettiest rooms in her parents' century-plus-old home, which was really saying something. They'd had it remodeled. Pale wood paneling matched the cabinets. White-and-silver marbled flooring matched the countertops. The stainless steel appliances were all new.

Her parents were her first and best financial planning clients. They'd retired a few years earlier from demanding yet fulfilling careers. Her mother had been a senior partner with a small architectural design company. Her father, Ramone Chase, had served as a senior policy analyst with the city's environmental protection agency. Zerleena continued to consult with them on strategies to maximize and reinvest their liquid assets as well and their retirement accounts.

She smiled at her father as he approached the sink. "Another great dinner, Dad. Thank you."

Aromas from their meal — baked chicken, stuffing, and broiled broccoli — lingered in the kitchen. Her parents were wonderful cooks and took turns preparing the family dinners. Zerleena was in charge of the dessert. Tonight's treat had been chocolate mousse.

"You're welcome." Ramone cleared the countertop, depositing the serving spoon and plate into the sink. His youthful physique, clothed in stone-washed black jeans and a gray Monarchs jersey, contradicted the dusting of white sprinkling his close-cropped hair. "I had to take your mother's cell phone away. Again."

Zerleena winced. "Thanks, Dad." Suppose her father hadn't disarmed her mother in time? Her body ice over with horror. She could only imagine what her mother would've said to Cornell if she'd gotten through to his show. "Mom, we've had this conversation. Many times. If you call into Cornell's program, you'll make the situation worse."

"How could it *possibly* get worse?" Jillian gestured with the pale orange sponge she'd been using to wipe the stovetop. "Have you heard the horrible things he's saying about you?"

More often than I care to remember.

Just the thought of Cornell was enough to make her blood boil. Zerleena drew a breath, determined to hold on to her happy mood. She loved her weekly dinners with her parents. They were a much nicer way of staying in touch than texts, emails, or phone calls. She didn't want to ruin the evening by invoking Cornell. However, she needed her mother understand, in this situation, the best way to help was to do nothing.

She picked up a sponge, which was a match to her mother's, and wiped the countertops. "Mom, I know the situation upsets you. I'm upset, too. The only advice I can give you is to stop listening to Cornell's show. You're boosting his ratings. He doesn't deserve to count you among his listeners."

Jillian's sigh must have been for effect. "Ignoring him won't make him go away, Leena."

Would anything short of an exorcism accomplish that?

Her professional contacts had assured her they could give her insight on her nemesis that could crush him. She was tempted, but responding to his idiocy would only fuel this feud of his own making. Cornell would get tired of her pretending he didn't exist. She was sure of it.

Zerleena wiped the countertop. Her mother cleaned the stovetop. They met at the sink. "I won't respond to him, Mom. If I engage, I'll be giving his lies credibility."

Jillian set down her sponge and pressed her fists against the warm brown slacks that covered her slim hips. Her expression was a mixture of frustration and concern. "Instead, he's taking your silence as consent for him to lie as much as he wants."

"Your mother's right, sweetheart." Her father's quiet words surprised her.

Her father had never before expressed his opinion

on how to handle the challenge that was Cornell. And she'd never asked him. For him to speak up now meant he also thought the situation had gone far enough.

She considered her parents. "If I was to respond, and I'm not convinced I should, what would you suggest I do?"

Jillian crossed her arms. Her hot pink nail polish matched her blouse. "You should call into his show and give him a set down he and his listeners will never forget. I've got some notes."

Zerleena caught her mother's forearm as Jillian started to walk past her presumably to get the notes she'd referenced.

"Mom, wait." Good grief. What had she gotten herself into? "Remember, I have a reputation to maintain. I can't lose control in public. That kind of display is hard to live down. The media would never let me forget it. Instead of, 'Zerleena Chase, *USAToday* and *New York Times* best-selling author and financial planner," I'll be, "Zerleena Chase, the woman who had a major meltdown on satellite radio.' For years."

"Leena." Jillian took a breath. This was serious. "I worked in a male-dominated industry. Do you think I got to be senior partner at an architectural firm by being diplomatic?"

Zerleena and Ramone exchanged a look. They'd seen her mother at work. In that environment, she was very different from the adoring wife and doting mother they knew and loved.

"In fairness, Jill, Leena's career is more public facing than yours had been." Ramone's lips twitched as he struggled with a smile.

"All right." Jillian inclined her head. "Then what would you suggest, Ray?"

Ramone's eyes were pensive. "I don't know yet. But I do know we have to be prepared to do something and soon. This isn't your overprotective father speaking. This is your number one fan. Cornell's attacks have gone unheeded long enough."

To handle Cornell, she'd need her mother's assertiveness and her father's stratagem. She didn't have either. Was it time to use the information she'd been collecting? Once she opened that file, there was no going back.

***

"Can we talk?" Marlon stopped less than an arm's length from Zerleena after waiting what seemed like hours for her to meet him in her condo building's lobby Thursday evening.

Zerleena closed her eyes briefly, but not before Marlon caught the flash of frustration in their brown depths. "You can't show up at my condo without notice. You're interrupting my work." Her command was an irritated hiss.

"This won't take long. I promise."

Concern softened her expression. Her eyes searched his. Did she see his agitation, his desperation? Without a word, Zerleena turned to lead him to the elevators that would carry them to her twenty-first floor condo. In the close confines of the elevator, Zerleena's soft scent – roses and powder – surrounded him. He shifted closer to her.

Their silence wore down his composure even further. Marlon glanced at his black Rolex. It was after five o'clock. "What are you working on?"

"My manuscript is due in a couple of weeks." Zerleena mumbled her response. It was as though she was reluctant to share with him even that small glimpse into her life. That tore at his heart.

Marlon tried to squeeze his way in. "How's it going?"

Zerleena shrugged restlessly. "Fine."

He didn't believe her. An uneasy silence stood between them until they arrived at her floor.

Zerleena let him into her condo. Once again, it offered the warm welcome she seemed determined to withhold. Its open floor plan and abundance of leafy green plants lifted his mood.

"What's on your mind?" Zerleena locked her door before leading him into her great room.

"That's a loaded question." Marlon waited until she faced him before allowing his gaze to travel over her.

He'd meant the look to be quick and teasing, but his body's response to her compelled him to linger. Her black slouchy sweater hinted at the fullness of her breasts. Marlon's palms heated as though he was holding them. Zerleena's silver yoga pants hugged her rounded hips and long shapely legs.

Marlon smiled when his eyes dropped to her fuzzy pale pink slipper socks with the pattern of dancing gray rabbits. "Nice socks."

"Can you please get to the point? I have a lot of work to do." Zerleena stance — hip cocked and fists on her waist — emphasized her alluring figure. Not helpful.

Marlon turned away so he could focus. Where did he start? Once he began, would he be able to stop? Was it smart to strip bare his fears and insecurities in front of Zerleena when he was trying to convince her to give him another chance?

"Marl?" Concern whispered in Zerleena's voice.

Marlon turned back to her. He saw the worry in her dark eyes. Coming to Zerleena had seemed like a good idea when his frustration was building. Now that it had boiled over, he wasn't as sure.

But Zerleena knew the real Marlon, the person he'd been before he'd created an NBA champion personae that neither competitors nor the media could pierce.

He crossed the mahogany flooring to the other side of the great room. Where should he being? "Did you see the game last night?"

"I don't watch basketball anymore."

Marlon spun to face her. She'd moved to stand a little more than an arm's length from him. "You *loved* basketball."

Zerleena hesitated. "Not anymore."

Marlon's eyes narrowed. He didn't believe her. Not for a minute. In college, she'd been a basketball fanatic, going nose to nose with him and anyone who dared to malign her beloved Brooklyn Monarchs. She'd whipped out rankings, team stats, players' personal records with photographic recall. That devotion had been unshakeable despite the Monarchs' struggling seasons. She'd stood strong even at their alma mater, Michigan State University, where most of her classmates had rooted for the Detroit Pistons.

But why would she lie to him? "What happened? Why did you stop enjoying the game?"

Mocking amusement gleamed in her eyes. "It didn't have anything to do with you so give your ego a rest." She shrugged. "There are more important things in life than basketball. But I heard the team lost."

The disappointment in knowing they no longer shared a love of basketball weighed him down. The chasm between them was widening. "I thought a game loss was hard before. It's even harder when you're coming off the bench after an entire career as a starter."

"I'm sure." Something flickered across her delicate features. Compassion? Empathy? It gave him hope. "But you got a lot of playing time."

Marlon frowned. "How do you know that if you didn't watch the game?"

Zerleena blinked. "It was on the local news."

Marlon accepted her explanation. For now. "I feel

like a thirty-seven-year-old rookie, starting from scratch." His laugh was dry and humorless.

"It's understandable this adjustment will be hard. There are a lot of new-to-you situations: the team, teammates, the city, coming off the bench."

Marlon wandered her great room, stopping to trace the elegantly simple candlesticks standing on her blonde wood fireplace mantel. Did she ever use them? How often — and with whom?

He continued on to touch the plants spreading across the bamboo and bronze shelving. The large picture windows beside them framed a vibrant view of Brooklyn's Prospect Park in autumn.

"The locker room has been tense. I didn't want to be traded and the Monarchs don't want me on their team." The words came with difficulty, but he needed to confide in someone. He needed to confide in her.

She may disagree, but Zerleena and DeMarcus were the only friends he had in Brooklyn. It wouldn't be fair to involve DeMarcus in his battle for the locker room. Zerleena was his only option. But even if he'd had a score of friends to choose from, he still would have ended up in her lobby.

"You're the Magnificent Marlon Burress." There was humor in Zerleena's tone. "You'll win them over – or you'll wear them down. Either way, the locker room will come to accept you."

"I'm not feeling so magnificent at the moment. What if I can't get the other players to accept me? Suppose I can't make a difference on the court? What if I end my career on a losing team with a losing record?" When he'd first arrived in Brooklyn, he'd hoped to impress Zerleena with his confidence and success. Instead, he was acting like a colicky baby. He disgusted himself.

Was she disgusted by him?

Marlon squeezed his eyes shut, dreading her response.

"I can't believe you. After all you've accomplished, how can you *still* underestimate yourself?"

Zerleena had always had faith in him, even when he hadn't believed in himself. Marlon turned, surprised to find her frowning at him in confusion. "I—"

She cut him off. "Do you realize only about one-point-two percent of NCAA men's basketball players make it to the NBA? And you made it, Marl. Did you know, as of the start of this season, six NBA franchises have never made it to the Finals? Three of those teams have never even won their conference."

As a student of the game, Marlon was aware of all that, but he didn't want to interrupt Zerleena. She was on a roll. And hearing those stats from her was more reassuring than repeating them to himself or hearing them from anyone else. It wasn't just the words; it was the person saying them. That passion for the game, a passion they'd shared. Why was she denying it now?

Zerleena continued. "You've always had the skills, drive, and determination to achieve whatever goals you've set. You just need to believe in yourself."

Marlon went still. Those words jerked him back through time to their junior year at Michigan State.

You have the skills, drive, and determination to achieve whatever you want, Marl. If the NBA is your goal, you'll make it. I believe in you.

The image was so vivid. He was back in Zerleena's drafty apartment, letting her faith fuel him. He could smell the popcorn — not burned — they'd snack on late at night. Her words had remained with him through graduation, the draft, and his first championship.

In that moment, he realized how much Zerleena had contributed to his successes. "Thank you, Leena."

She surveyed the room as though looking for something. "You're welcome." She glanced at her Apple iWatch.

Marlon stepped forward, hoping to distract her from the time. He wasn't ready to leave. Not yet. "The Monarchs aren't getting along with each other, either. They're back to being the league's most dysfunctional team."

"Which explains why they lost so badly last night." Zerleena rolled her eyes with disgust. "You have your work cut out for you, but Jaclyn Jones wouldn't have traded for you if she didn't think the team needed you."

"Thanks, Leena. Talking with you has helped clear my mind and put things in perspective." The knots in Marlon's back and shoulders eased. He managed a real smile.

Zerleena's gaze bounced away from his. That smile still had the power to disarm and distract her. "To further put things in perspective, you have a degree in broadcast journalism. Plenty of sports networks — TV and radio — would be thrilled to have the Marvelous Marlon Burress on their lineup."

He gave her a sexy crooked smile. "That had sounded like a good idea when I was twenty-two. Now I'm not so sure I can be that close to the court without being on it."

"It's something to think about." She sensed him slipping back into brooding tension. Time to change the subject. "In the spirit of our newfound friendship, I know you're still getting used to Brooklyn. If you don't already have plans for Thanksgiving, my parents and I would be happy for you to join us."

Marlon's eyes brightened at the invitation. His smile was slow and easy. "Thanks but I'm spending Thanksgiving with my parents in Miami. I'm flying down after the Raptors game in Toronto and coming back in time for our home game against the Sixers."

"That's wonderful. How are your parents?" Zerleena didn't know what she felt, relief or disappointment. But she was certain she didn't want to examine her reaction too closely.

"They're fine. Thanks for asking. They claim to miss me, but not enough to move to Brooklyn."

Zerleena grinned. "I'm sure they're looking forward to spending the holiday with you."

"They are, which makes me suspect they have a list of chores for me to help with." Marlon chuckled.

Zerleena had spent a lot of time with Marlon's parents during her undergraduate years. Carl and Delia Burress had attended all of Marlon's college games, home and away. She liked them. They were warm, funny, and caring. "I can understand their not wanting to uproot the life they've created for themselves: their home, friends, and hangouts."

"I get it. It's just that I miss them."

"I'm sure you do. You're a very close family."

He glanced at his watch. "I should leave so you can get back to work."

"Yes. Deadlines." Her shrug was apologetic.

"Of course. I'm sorry for interrupting you." Marlon followed her to her door.

"No problem. I'm glad I could help. It's what friends are for." She held the door open for him.

Marlon stopped close beside her and inhaled her scent. The muscles in his groin tightened. He fought the urge to kiss her goodbye. "Good luck with your writing. Thanks again for being a friend when I needed one."

"You're welcome."

Marlon nodded. He let his gaze caress her features before coaxing his legs to move. He wandered to the elevator banks, then pressed the button to call the car that would take him back to the lobby.

Zerleena's faith that he could win over the locker room bolstered his confidence and gave him hope that his season wouldn't be a total nightmare. But what about them? What could he hope for their relationship? Friendship was fine. For now. But he wanted more from her. So much more. Could he find a reason to hope for a chance to win back the only woman he could ever love?

***

"If *I* were dating a Monarchs player, I'd be screaming about it from the rooftops." The caller shouted into the listener line during the second hour of Zerleena's She Shed.

Zerleena sent a startled look to D.C. seated on the other side of her sound room. D.C. also looked taken aback. Although most of the listener questions had been related to the show's format of budgets and investing, D.C. had sent her a written note that she was fielding far too many comments and inquiries about Marlon during the twenty-minute question-and-answer portion of their three-hour program. Had this caller deliberately misrepresented her intent in order to slip past D.C.'s screening?

"Thank you for your comment, Kat from Brooklyn." Zerleena disconnected the call. "Just a reminder, ladies — and I know a few gentlemen tune into the She Shed as well — we're only taking calls on this morning's topic, which is rebalancing your portfolio during a down market. Let's hear only from people with questions or comments about that, please. D.C., who do we have next?"

Thankfully, the next three callers stayed on topic. Zerleena once again relaxed in the more familiar territory of reallocations and debt reductions. "We have time for one more call. Who's on the line, D.C.?"

"Roxanne from Queens has a question about joint retirement accounts." D.C. pressed a couple of buttons to route the call to Zerleena's on-air system.

Zerleena picked up the call. "Hi, Roxanne from Queens. What's your question about joint retirement accounts?"

"I just said that to get through. Why're you being so cagey about dating Marlon Burress?" Roxanne whispered into the phone. "You're a public figure. We have a right to ask about your love life."

Zerleena briefly squeezed her eyes shut. "No, Roxanne. You don't have a right to ask that. But to set the record straight, I'm not dating Marlon Burress."

Roxanne made a tsking sound. "How d'you mean you aren't dating him? You were photographed outside of that fancy Italian restaurant. Everyone knows Italian is a date food."

"I didn't know that." The first stirrings of a headache brushed across her right temple. "Thank you for your call, Roxanne." Zerleena disconnected. She glanced at the digital wall clock to her right. For the few minutes left to her show, it was probably safest to avoid calls. "And thank you to everyone for tuning in today. Mark your calendars for my upcoming book, *Financial Wisdom from the She Shed*, which is scheduled for release January of next year." Still one minute left. Zerleena spoke slowly. "Preorder your copy and make plans to start next year on the right financial footing. Thanks again, everyone, for listening. Enjoy your weekend. D.C. and I will see you bright and early Monday morning. Until then, spend wisely."

D.C. joined her in the narrow hallway outside of their sound booths. "That was so not brave of you."

Zerleena exhaled a sharp breath. "Those callers were getting out of control. You heard that last one. She lied so she could get on the air to ask about Marlon."

"She's not the only one who'd like to know." D.C. muttered the comment. Her long gold-and-brown-patterned sweater dress had a loose brown faux leather belt that made her waist look tiny.

Zerleena rolled her eyes, then turned to lead them back to their office. "I don't get up before the crack of dawn and drag myself to the station in the dark to talk about Marlon Burress."

"Would sharing a little of your personal life be such a bad thing?"

"I do talk about my personal life."

"Your investment habits and savings goals don't qualify as personal." D.C.'s comeback was as dry as dust.

She strode past D.C.'s desk on the way to her own. "I bet Marlon is behind those disruptive calls."

They were invasive, just the kind of thing Marlon

would orchestrate to make sure she was thinking about him.

It's been fifteen years. If I haven't stopped thinking about him yet, when will I?

"You think Burress somehow arranged for people to call in to talk about him?"

"I wouldn't put it past him." But she'd heard D.C.'s incredulous tone. Was she being unfair? With a mental shrug, she settled behind her desk.

"That sounds a little extra, don't you think? This guy has really gotten to you."

It was frustrating to admit, but D.C. was right. Marlon had gotten to her, just as she'd feared he would. After his surprise appearance Thursday night, she hadn't been able to write a single decent paragraph. She kept reliving their conversation. The vulnerability he'd shown had reminded Zerleena so clearly of the younger man she'd fallen in love with.

The one who'd broken my heart.

"We want to know more about *you*." D.C. had continued talking while Zerleena had been visiting her past. "It's natural that people who've been following your work for so long would be curious about you. Are you dating? Do you have pets? What do you do when you're not counting your money?"

"If you think it's a good idea to include some of that information, then fine I'll work it in." She was tired of fighting what appeared to be the inevitable.

D.C. grinned. "Great! And maybe we should invite Burress onto the show."

"Oh, no. No way. That's going too far."

"Come on, Leena. Your callers would love it."

"Marlon has nothing to do with this show."

"But your listeners want to know about him."

"Then they can tune into sports radio."

D.C. sat forward on her chair. "We don't have to interview him about sports. We could ask him about his investments, his retirement strategies. You've been talking about interviewing Jaclyn Jones. Why can't we talk with Burress?"

Zerleena wanted to channel her inner mom and respond with, *Because I said so.*

"Our show focuses on the *woman's* perspective on investing. I want our listeners to identify with our guests."

"We can interview both. Speaking with Burress will allow listeners to compare and contrast the male and female perspectives."

Zerleena paused over D.C.'s suggestion. It was a good one. Maybe they could use a different male perspective like Warrick Evans's or Vincent Jardine's.

Did she want to open another part of her life to Marlon? The idea of showing him how well she'd done despite his breaking her heart did appeal to her. Then he'd see how far she'd traveled from his shadow — and she was never going back.

"D.C., I'm not bringing Marlon onto my show."

Chapter 7

"Two games. Two losses." Friday night, DeMarcus's gaze scorched the visiting team's locker room in Madison Square Garden like a Slacker Seeking Missile. "We're playing the Celtics tomorrow at home. Care to make it three for three?"

Neither Marlon nor any of the other players volunteered an answer to DeMarcus's rhetorical question.

The New York Knicks had just shellacked the Monarchs. Marlon was sick to his stomach. The Knicks had never let up — even after it was clear several of the Monarchs had. The final score had been 105 to 79. Looking at the scoreboard had almost made his eyes bleed. Had he ever played for a team — high school, college, or pros — that had lost that badly? It was a twenty-six-point spread.

No.

Racking up back-to-back losses was bad. Hosting a demoralizing display on one's home court in front of one's fans would be worse. They couldn't allow that to happen tomorrow night.

DeMarcus continued in the same tight voice. "I've seen neighborhood pick-up games with players who bring more of a commitment than what you brought tonight. What the hell happened to you in the off-season?"

Marlon rubbed his hand over his brow. He wasn't used to being berated by a coach. But then, he wasn't used to playing on such a dismal team. It was even harder to hear that tone and those words from a former teammate he'd admired. "We didn't pass the ball, Coach."

"You don't speak for us." Anthony ground the words through clenched teeth.

Marlon eyed the other man. Was St. Anthony crazy? That could explain his game decisions. "Look, man, like it or not, I'm on this team. I have the same right to speak as you do."

Anthony jabbed a finger at Marlon. "I *don't* like you being on my team, and you haven't *earned* the right to speak for us."

"Stop!" DeMarcus's command brought a decisive end to Anthony's schoolyard squabbling. He looked around the room. "This is the same bullshit you brought last season. I'm only saying this once: You're a team. Play like it."

The "or else" may not have been spoken, but Marlon was certain they'd all heard it.

The locker room was silent as DeMarcus marched out. The controlled snick of the door closing demonstrated the control he exerted over his temper. Scary.

Marlon turned to the other players. "What's it going to take to get you clowns to start passing the ball to me? Is there a secret code? A magic phrase or something? Should I say 'please'?"

Most of the Monarchs, including Warrick and Barron, didn't acknowledge his question. Vincent and Serge looked at him, then turned away to continue dressing. Anthony started to speak, but Jamal cut him off.

"Who're you calling clowns, fool?" The wiry shooting guard stood bare-chested in front of his locker. His dark gaze blasted venom at Marlon from across the room. "The only one getting laughs on that court tonight was you."

"You sure about that?" Marlon's muscles were so tight, he imaged he could hear them popping as he pulled his sage green sweater over his head. "Cause the way you were stumbling around the court, I'm pretty sure you were asleep. How could you have heard anything?"

Baller Basics 101: Get a good night's sleep before a game. What was preventing Jamal from doing that? The kid didn't seem to have a substance abuse problem. It must be his honey keeping him up late.

"There's plenty of blame for this loss to go around." Warrick's quiet words came from beside Marlon.

The veteran player tucked his button-down shirt into his slacks, going from baller to business man. Marlon couldn't lay any blame on Warrick for the Monarchs' pathetic play. As usual, one of the oldest players on the roster had carried the team on his back.

Marlon had no idea how the other man could still be standing.

"I don't agree with you, Rick." Marlon crossed his arms over his chest. "The few touches I got came from you passing me the ball so I don't see how any of this loss can be my fault."

Anthony stood from the bench in front of his locker. "You're going to hold yourself blameless? I thought you said you were part of this team?"

"And you said I wasn't. Which is it?" Marlon curled one corner of his lip. The other player was really starting to get on his nerves.

"You're not." Anthony's expression grew colder. "You aren't one of us. You don't belong on this team."

Vincent's laugh was sarcastic. "Hey, Saint Anthony—"

Anthony rounded on Vincent. "Am I going to have to go through another whole season with that stupid nickname?"

"Yes." Vincent arched his eyebrows. "Hey, *Saint Anthony*, you know the Bible so well. What does it say about strangers in a strange land?"

Anthony glared at Jamal. "Burress brought this on himself with his uncharitable attitude toward Rick."

Barron snorted as he finished putting on his shoes. "That's a good one, Tony. It's almost funny. Marlon was our conference championship opponent. The bullshit he dished on the court was low." Barron glanced pointedly at Marlon before turning back to Anthony. "But you're Rick's teammate. How do you explain the crap you gave him in the locker room in the post-season?"

Anthony paled. His gaze dropped to the cement flooring.

Warrick shrugged into his suitcoat before facing the room. He met the gaze of each teammate in turn. "What happened last season is between me and Marlon. I'm over it. Don't use it as an excuse to play like 13 individuals. We know what we can do when we play like a team. So play like a team."

Without another word, Warrick collected his gym bag and exited the locker room.

"Rick Evans is a classy dude." Marlon studied the closed door.

Warrick had been under a lot of pressure on and off the court last season. His teammates had been jealous of the media giving all the credit for the Monarchs' Cinderella season to the shooting guard. The other players — with the exception of Vincent and Barron — had taken out their resentment on Warrick, criticizing him during their media interviews and freezing him out on the court. There also had been a scandal involving a fan that had almost ended Warrick's marriage to Dr. Marilyn DeVry-Evans.

"I wouldn't have forgiven you." Jamal's tone was mean.

"No doubt." Marlon was unfazed. He swung his gym bag onto his shoulder. "I wonder if he's forgiven you." He started toward the door.

Anthony's voice stopped him. "It's very immature of you to always need to have the last word."

"Yes, it is." Marlon tossed a cocky grin over his shoulder before leaving the room.

He exhaled as he made his way to the parking lot and the bus service that would take the Monarchs to John F. Kennedy International Airport. The league rumors had been right: The Monarchs were worse than a bunch of colicky babies. Could he survive the next eight months?

***

Between two-point-three and two-point-six-million people lived in the New York City borough of Brooklyn. All of them must be in Prospect Park this Sunday morning. Marlon couldn't blame them. For late fall, the weather was comfortably crisp, perfect for an early morning run.

He completed his second lap around the park's almost three-and-a-half-mile pedestrian loop. Without stopping, he turned toward the Eastern Parkway Boulevard entrance to jog to his car. Weaving through and around the crowd of other runners, walkers, cyclists, and meanderers, he exited the park, then threaded through the shoppers milling around the farmer's market. Good practice for maneuvering his way past defenders on the basketball court.

In his peripheral vision, he noticed stares and double takes from some of the people he blew past on his way out of the park. His recognition in the Monarchs town was growing. Would it translate to acceptance? He'd heard boos and jeers from the Monarchs faithful each time he'd taken their home court. Again, that's not the way he'd imagined finishing his career. But then, he'd never spent much time picturing his retirement. He'd always been more focused on either the game he was in or the one he was about to play.

Four blocks later, Marlon arrived at his three-year-old luxury SUV. His lips curved as he once again considered how out of place his green vehicle looked among the black, silver, and gray cars in the Monarchs practice facility's lot.

Marlon slowed to walk to the end of the block and back as part of his cool-down before driving home. As he started his SUV, his cell rang almost on cue. His agent's name popped onto his caller ID. It wasn't unusual for Jett to contact him on a Sunday. Maybe the former player was about to repay Marlon's loyalty with a ticket out of Brooklyn.

Marlon answered his phone through his car's Bluetooth. "Jett, what're you hearing?"

Had his agent heard his desperate plea for help? Marlon checked his mirrors before extricating his car from the too small parking spot and onto the road.

"A lot. I've been working on catching up on my emails." The only times Jett sounded this excited was when he'd been able to negotiate a better contract. Dare he hope Jett had news about a trade?

"So tell me."

"How do you know Zerleena Chase?"

Why was everyone asking him about Zerleena? "We went to college together." And had fallen in love. "Why?"

"I got a call from Cornell Redd, he's a financial adviser and host of Reddy to Earn on satellite radio. He's based in Brooklyn." Beneath Jett's Southern accent, rustling sounds indicated he was sifting through papers on his desk. Jett liked to write things down in addition to saving the information in his computer.

"What does this have to do with my being traded out of Brooklyn?" Marlon stopped to check traffic before crossing a surprisingly empty intersection.

"It doesn't have anything to do with your contract, at least not directly. But it has a lot to do with an opportunity to raise your profile in Brooklyn, which will go a long way toward getting other teams to look at you favorably. You know teams want players who would fit in with their franchise and the community."

Marlon snorted. "Then what am I doing in Brooklyn? Jaclyn Jones picked up my contract even though I played for her franchise's rival."

"Jaclyn Jones is a pragmatic businesswoman. She must've seen something in your game that her team needed." There was a shrug in Jett's voice.

Marlon stopped at a corner, scowling absently at a traffic light. "And what's that? Did she think I looked pretty sitting on a bench?"

"Marl, you're getting a lot of playing time." Jett's long-suffering sigh didn't make Marlon feel better.

Neither did his placating words. "Listen, Redd wants to book you on his show."

Marlon's eyebrows jumped up his forehead. Zerleena had told him the satellite radio host would contact him and she'd been right. Cornell wanted to interview him even though Marlon had no business experience or financial expertise to speak of.

Why was Cornell so desperate to get information about Zerleena and Marlon's relationship? Marlon didn't believe it was because Cornell was a business rival, as Zerleena had claimed. What was the other man's real interest in her?

Whatever it was, Marlon wasn't going to play along. "I'm not interested." His response was met with a surprised silence.

"Why not? Redd sounds really interested in talking with you."

Marlon turned onto his street. "Yeah, he wants to ask me a bunch of questions about Leena. How does that get me out of Brooklyn?"

"There's no immediate benefit, but it shows you're building ties with the community."

Marlon rolled his eyes as he drove into his condo building's underground parking garage. "Leena's a friend." And he didn't have many in this town. "He and Leena are competitors. I'm not playing his game."

"This is business." Jett's argument had worked in the past. It wasn't working this time. "As a friend, she'll understand."

Marlon almost laughed. "You don't know her. Besides, I promised I wouldn't go on Redd's show."

"Why did you do that?"

Marlon guided his car around the garage. "Did I mention Leena and I are friends?"

"Funny, you've never mentioned her to me before. I'd have remembered if you'd told me you knew Zerleena Chase. My wife loves her."

Marlon felt a burst of pride. Zerleena had built an impressive career for herself. In addition to being a business mogul, she also was a philanthropist. He wished he'd been here to watch her achieve her goals.

"Does your wife know you're trying to talk me into going on her rival's show?"

Jett sighed. "This could be good publicity for her, too. If Redd wants to spend his valuable airtime talking about his competitor, let him."

Marlon pulled into his assigned parking spot and aimed a skeptical look toward the garage's cement wall. Had Jett lost his mind? "How would it be good for Leena to have this clown talk smack about her on his show? No, I'm not doing it, Jett. Come up with something else."

"Marl—"

"You're not changing my mind." Marlon turned off his car's engine and pressed back against his soft, cloth seat. "I gave my word."

"This isn't a post-game conference. You don't have to answer Redd's questions. You can control the interview."

Marlon paused. He'd control of the interview? "Then I decide how to answer his questions?"

"That's right."

This opened more possibilities for another shot at changing Zerleena's mind about him. "All right. I'll do it. You know my schedule. Set something up."

Marlon climbed out of his SUV and into the role of Zerleena's hero. It felt good.

***

"You came all by yourself tonight, Zerleena? No date? How ... unsurprising." Cornell took the seat beside her at the awards banquet table Thursday evening.

Zerleena frowned at her nemesis, taking in the striking image he made in his navy suit, cream shirt, and matching bow tie. It was too bad his beauty was only skin deep. "That seat's taken."

She'd made sure in advance Cornell wouldn't be seated at her table for this three-hour event. His pompous company would have done more to ruin the banquet for her than the tasteless chicken and boiled carrots dinner.

Who came up with these menus and why did they dislike people?

It also wouldn't be a bad idea for the hotel to turn up the temperature a degree or ten. Why were banquet rooms always so cold?

Cornell gave her his dimpled smile. His strawberry

blond hair shone beneath the fluorescent lights as he inclined his head across the room. "Jeff and I are old friends. I told him I wanted to sit beside you."

Zerleena scanned the room as she washed away the bitter taste of frustration with her iced tea. The area was small enough to make the event seem packed. The space was bright with pale plasterboard walls, and cream and blue accents in the carpeting.

Jeffrey Engelmann had moved to a table toward the back where he was engaged in conversation with several of the people surrounding him. He seemed to be having fun, almost as though he belonged there.

Her muscles shook with aggravation. Zerleena was hyper aware of the six other people at their table. She suspected at least a couple of them were trying to eavesdrop on her conversation despite their apparent disinterest. Taking a deeper drink of her iced tea, she held onto her control with both fists.

Beneath the scent of butter and dinner rolls, she caught a whiff of Cornell's cologne. He smelled like the beach. She lowered her voice. "Why do I have the feeling you arranged this?"

"I have no idea what you're talking about." He shook his head as though he was clueless. But the mocking look in his sociopathic gray eyes and the smile ghosting his thin lips exposed his lie.

She was tired of men lying to her. "Stop playing games. What do you want?"

"I'm surprised you're here alone. I'd've thought you'd bring a date since you were nominated for an award in the Best Informational Programming category." Cornell's words held mockery — and envy. "You look beautiful, by the way."

Zerleena frowned. He said that every time he saw her. Did he think flattery would gain him anything? He was wrong. It only made her distrust him more.

"*You're* here alone." She turned away from him, intending to engage another tablemate in conversation. Perhaps the jovial woman who hosted a do-it-yourself auto repair program.

But Cornell refused to be ignored. "I'm not dating an NBA player."

Zerleena's guts froze. Cornell's voice had carried beyond the two of them. Now their other tablemates dropped their pretense and were openly listening. She sensed them evaluating her appearance in her simple-but-elegant black dress, which she'd accessorized with matching jewelry: a chunky onyx bracelet, necklace, and earrings. Did she fit their image of an NBA player's girlfriend, whatever that looked like? She could care less.

Right?

At least her rising temper had the benefit of warming her in the frozen tundra the hotel hilariously called a ballroom. She lowered her voice, stripping it of inflection. "You went to a lot of trouble to sit at my table. Why?"

"I've said it before: We'd make a great team." Cornell's smile widened in his broad white face. He searched her features. "I know you disagree, but I really think you should consider it. You could benefit by expanding your audience beyond just the female market."

Was he trying to push her buttons?

Did she need to ask?

Zerleena arched an eyebrow. "Men attend my workshops, listen to my show, and buy my books. You have my answer. It won't change. Ever."

"It should." Cornell leaned forward as though trying to be discreet — in the middle of a crowded ballroom at a table set for eight. "You're developing a reputation as a man hater."

She gave him a patronizing smile. "I don't hate *men*, Cornell. I dislike *you*, which is one of the many reasons I'll never go into business with you."

"Working together, we'd increase our exposure."

"I already have a much bigger platform than you." She shrugged her shoulders, savoring every word she'd earned the right to say. "I have more best-selling books, more sold-out workshops, and more than twice as many listeners. My social media following alone eclipses yours. You'd be reaping all the benefits of what *I'd* bring to the table. What could I gain from working with *you*?"

Cornell's face flushed. His gaze swept the table as though desperate to know whether anyone had heard her. He'd chosen the place and time. He'd then pushed when she'd warned him to back off. Some men thought they knew everything. They couldn't listen. They had to be taught. Repeatedly.

"Your boyfriend's going to be on my show." Cornell's eyes glinted with satisfaction.

"What are you talking about?" Zerleena knew he was referring to Marlon. She gritted her teeth to keep from shouting Marlon wasn't her boyfriend. Not anymore. Not for a very long time.

"Marlon Burress, as you well know. His agent's helping me set it up." Cornell's tone was confident. "The guy sounded excited when I told him I wanted to talk with your boyfriend about your relationship."

Zerleena was glad she'd asked Marlon not to get involved in Cornell's campaign against her. He'd given her his word he wouldn't.

She surreptitiously looked around the table. Her companions' interest in her conversation with Cornell didn't seem to have waned. Darn it.

She tilted her head and gave Cornell a speculative look. "For a show that claims to provide financial advice, you spend a lot of time talking about personal relationships, mine in particular. Why is that?"

Cornell shrugged. "Women see you as a role model, but you're giving them the impression the only way for them to achieve financial success is to live like a nun."

"That's not true."

"I've asked you out more than once and you keep turning me down."

She snorted a laugh. "That doesn't mean I don't have a personal life. It shows I have standards."

"Ouch. That hurt." Cornell's wounded expression

seemed faked. "Anyway, I guess we'll find out how much of a social life you have when I interview Burress."

"Did Marlon commit to a date for the interview?" Zerleena knew Marlon wouldn't break his word. Yes, it had been fifteen years. How could she forget? But he wouldn't have changed that much.

A flicker of doubt winked across Cornell's features before disappearing. "Not yet."

Zerleena couldn't restrain a smug smile. "Then you don't have an interview."

"We'll see." He didn't sound as confident as he tried to appear.

"I already have." She was enjoying this. Marlon had always kept his word to her. When he'd promised his team would make the NCAA playoffs, they had. When he'd said he was leaving her behind, he had. Why would Cornell be any different?

***

They were going to lose. Again.

Marlon didn't want to believe it, but he couldn't deny the evidence in front of his eyes. At least they weren't losing at home. Again. No, this Friday night road loss to the Boston Celtics was coming to Monarchs players and fans straight from TD Garden.

He closed his eyes, but the image of Jamal's air ball — one of many during this game alone — would revisit him in his nightmares.

The Monarchs had been hurting themselves all night. Marlon shifted on his seat again. He had a photo-perfect view of their self-inflicted wounds from his position near the Monarchs basket. He'd been sidelined for most of the fourth quarter. Now the game clock was counting down to the final seconds of the Monarchs' sixth game — their fifth loss. Monday night, they'd beaten the Chicago Bulls at home by a tenuous five points.

Anthony grabbed the ball after the Celtics scored – again - and raced back down the court, spinning and weaving between Celtics defenders.

"*Tony*! Serge is *open*!" The tips of DeMarcus's black Italian loafers almost touched the sideline. He gestured toward the post where the French giant from Lourdes had distanced himself from Celtics Robert Williams III, another towering Frenchman. "Get the ball to Serge!"

Marlon dragged both hands over his head as Anthony either didn't hear or chose to ignore their coach. He didn't pass the ball. He didn't signal his teammates into position. He was playing for himself, as were Serge and Jamal.

At the post, Anthony tried to take the ball over Jaylen Brown, the Celtics' six-six guard. He missed. Brown didn't even have to work for the rebound. He just snatched it from the air as the Monarchs jogged to the other end of the court. With even less effort, he led the Celtics back up court for a laughably easy layup. Two points; 103-98, Celtics.

Marlon straightened on his seat and crossed his arms. He grabbed a chunk of his upper arm and pinched. Hard. He winced at the pain. No, this wasn't a nightmare. It was his new reality.

Unbelievable.

Warrick fought his way under the basket. He snatched the rebound. Marlon felt his frustration. The game clock read thirty seconds and counting. The shot clock flashed seventeen seconds. The arena was loud with the shouts of "Defense!"

Marlon snorted. As though the Celtics needed the encouragement. They'd been playing defense and offense just fine all night. The Monarchs were the ones who couldn't cobble together either one.

Warrick shouted a play to Jamal. Marlon knew the scheme would place the younger man at the left perimeter of the Celtics' basket. Jamal rolled his eyes and sprinted to the post. Warrick's features stiffened with impatience. Marlon's palms itched with the need to storm the court and smack the second-year player into next Sunday.

The shot clock shut off. The game clock counted down from twenty-two seconds. Vincent extended his hands for the ball. Warrick tossed it to him before positioning himself at the left perimeter. Celtics guards Garrison Mathews and Josh Richardson double teamed him as they had all night. Warrick had been fighting the Celtics as well as his teammates for the entire game.

Marlon shifted once more on his seat. He wanted

the game to end. He needed it to end. He glanced at DeMarcus. His new head coach seemed to be looking for a miracle. With seventeen seconds left to the game, he'd better pray faster.

The Monarchs found positions near the Celtics' basket, drawing their defenders with them. Brown stayed with Anthony in the paint. Celtics center Enes Kanter shadowed Vincent's advance from center court. Williams followed Serge to the right perimeter. Jamal stood wide open at the post.

A pass to Jamal would make an easy layup. A gift. The game would end with a more respectable score. But that was too much to ask of Jamal. The two-year veteran had shown he was more interested in style points than game points. Marlon willed Vincent to brave the triangle defense and take the ball to the post himself.

Please. Please. Please.

Vincent ignored Marlon's silent entreaty. He kicked the ball to Jamal. Jamal stepped back and spun, an unnecessary performance. His lack of focus allowed the Celtics to abandon their coverage of Jamal's teammates and converge on the hapless guard.

The Celtics stripped the ball from Jamal as easily as taking candy from a baby. Williams came up with the possession. He rocketed across the court as the game clock ticked down seven, six, five ...

From the three-point arc, Williams centered himself before taking the shot. The ball arced in the air.

The buzzer sounded. The ball hit the rim, then bounced through the net. Three points.

Final score: Celtics 106, Monarchs 98.

Marlon sprang from his seat. He couldn't handle much more of this. It had to end. But what could he do from the bench?

Chapter 8

The tension in the visiting team's locker room was thicker than the soles of his sneakers. Its weight pressed down on Marlon's shoulders like a king-sized mattress. He cast a glare around the room. He and the other players were dressing. In less than half an hour, the bus would be ready to take them to the airport for the flight back to Brooklyn. The room smelled of soap and an abundance of Jamal's cologne, leather and seaweed. Marlon breathed gingerly.

"So, Monarchs." He set his sights on Jamal as he broke the silence. "Are you working on winning any more games this season or is that one W we posted Monday all there is?"

Jamal erupted as Marlon had anticipated. He slammed the door to the locker he was using. The slap of metal on metal echoed around the room. "Man, why don't you shut your stupid mouth? Just shut the hell up."

"Why don't you listen? You go out on the court like every game's The Jamal Ward Show. Maybe The Jamal Ward Shit Show. And no one wants to see that." Marlon gave the young player his signature smile, a little amused, a bit mean.

Jamal stepped back. "Well, at least I'm on the court." His voice was more bluster.

"Yes, you're on the court. Losing. Games." Marlon glanced at the eight other players who came off the bench behind the starters. Most were ignoring Jamal, including Barron. But one or two shook their heads or rolled their eyes at his comment.

He turned back to Jamal. "You know basketball is a *team* sport, right? That's my point. You don't play like you're on a team. Neither do you." He pointed at Serge. "Or you." He shifted his finger to Anthony. "I was on the bench, and you know what I saw? Five teams on the court." He spread the fingers of his right hand and counted off. "Celtics. Tony. Serge. Jamal. And then Rick and Vinny. They're the only ones working together. What's wrong with the rest of you? Coach G said play like a team. Why can't you do that?"

Serge crossed his arms over his bare chest. The six-foot-ten starting forward wore his dark blond hair pulled straight back in a shoulder length ponytail. His lean square features were clean shaven. His blue eyes were sharp. "You come here and try to criticize the way we play. Maybe we don't like the way you play."

Marlon shrugged. "Okay. Let's talk about that. What's wrong with my game?"

Serge waved a hand dismissively toward Marlon. "You do too much trash talking. You like to rile up our opponents. They try to fight you and get into foul trouble."

Marlon nodded. "That's right. We lost to the Celtics

by eight points. If it wasn't for those free throws, we'd've lost by more."

"You don't know that." Anthony shouted his interruption. "You're the one pissing off the player, but once you're back on the bench, he and his teammates take it out on us. Throwing elbows and arms. That's bull, man. You need to stop that shit."

"Yeah!" Jamal jerked his chin up. "You think you're the Bad Boy of Basketball or something. You're just a punk."

"All right. You want me to mind my manners. That's fine." Marlon arched an eyebrow. "Now what are you going to do to play like a team?"

He'd always done whatever it took to win, whether it was flopping — before it was banned — or smack talking to get into his opponent's head. If these losers were ever going to win another game, they'd need all the tools in his toolbox: his defense, his offense, and his attitude. But if they wanted him to learn some manners, fine, he'd do it. New team, new rules.

"You see a lot from the bench." Warrick's quiet words stopped the noise in the locker room and cut across the conversation in Marlon's head.

"Yeah, man." Marlon turned to face Warrick's back. He sensed tension beneath the other player's serene demeanor. "I saw you and Tony trying to direct the plays from the court, and Marc's direction from the sidelines. These clowns ignored all three of you."

Something about Warrick reminded him of DeMarcus. The two were the only bright spots on this dysfunctional team. Like their head coach, Warrick was a born leader. He didn't speak much. It was more in his example. He brought intelligence and intensity to his game.

The dude knew what it took to win. Game after game, he strapped the team on his back and left everything on the court. In return, he was playing with a bunch of ball hogs who seem to have forgotten how they got their championship ring last season.

The veteran player was about Marlon's age, but didn't seem concerned about retirement. Was that because he was happily married?

Warrick turned, knotting his tie as he faced Marlon. "What did you do about what you saw?"

Marlon frowned. "What d'you mean?"

"While you were on the sideline watching us, what did you do to help us win?" Irritation and impatience snapped in Warrick's brown eyes but his voice remained level, almost unnaturally calm. "Did you cheer when we scored? Did you rally us when we turned the ball over? Did you call out things we may not have seen? What did you do?"

Marlon felt the heat of shame rising up his neck. "I didn't do anything."

"Thanks for recognizing that." Warrick grabbed his gym bag from his bench. "We all have things to work on and improve if we're going to get back to the finals. We need to play like a team, all thirteen of us for all four quarters, whether we're on the court or on the bench."

Marlon watched Warrick leave the locker room before grabbing his own bag and heading toward the parking lot. He was ashamed to admit it, but the other man was right. He'd spent the past six games thinking about what the other players had to do. He hadn't considered he wasn't acting as a member of the team, either.

Part of him couldn't accept that he was a Monarch. They'd been his division rival his entire career. Would he be able to get past that? Or would he rather be traded?

***

"Hey, Reddy to Earners! Do I have a treat for you today!" Cornell opened his satellite radio program, Reddy to Earn, with that provocative promise Monday afternoon.

Zerleena looked up from her dinner of blackened chicken salad and grape juice. "Hmm. Wonder if Corny is actually going to focus on financial management on his financial management program. Now that *would* be a treat."

Unable to hear her, Cornell continued. "Our guest today is none other than the newest player on our local NBA team, Marlon Burress, formerly of the Miami Waves but now with the Brooklyn Monarchs."

"What?" A mouthful of Zerleena's chicken salad went down the wrong pipe. A coughing fit seized her.

Seconds later, after regaining control, Zerleena

wiped tears from her cheeks. She stared wide-eyed at the icon of Cornell's show on her cell. This time, the betrayal was hotter and sharper than a blade. The first time Marlon had betrayed her by running off to the NBA and leaving her behind, it had hurt. But there hadn't been any promises between them. She'd hoped for forever, but they'd been college sweethearts and school was over. This time ... This time, there'd been a promise.

And Marlon had broken it.

Zerleena sat straight on her blonde wood kitchen chair. She shoved her salad aside. The spicy aroma of the blackened chicken no longer stirred her appetite. She glared at her phone as though she could see straight through its screen to Marlon's handsome, deceitful face.

Cornell continued his introduction. "If you've managed to read past the financial section of the newspaper to its sports pages, you probably know already today's very honored and accomplished guest is a fifteen-year veteran of professional basketball. In fact, he's an NBA MVP and two-time NBA champion. Marlon — may I call you Marlon?"

"Of course." Marlon's smooth, warm honey voice made Zerleena's heart flutter — and her fury burn.

It really was him. It was Marlon. On Cornell's show. The host wasn't lying. She shook her head and pried her fingers from their figurative grip on denial.

Cornell chuckled like a star-struck prepubescent. "Thank you and welcome to the show."

"Thanks for the invitation." Marlon's response made Zerleena ground additional millimeters from her teeth.

Her face flushed. Her nostrils flared. She wanted to pound something. Why was he doing this? Why would he help Cornell tear down her reputation? Surely, Marlon knew that was the only reason Cornell had invited him onto his show?

Zerleena waited through the preliminary question-and-answer part of Cornell's program. Her muscles tightened with each passing second as Cornell asked Marlon about his professional career, and his many and varied athletic accolades and achievements. Zerleena had followed Marlon's career. She was aware of all the accolades Cornell mentioned and ones he probably didn't have time to discuss.

A cloud of regret entered her bright and cheery kitchen. It wrapped around her, bringing a chill to her skin. She wished she'd been beside him to help celebrate his achievements.

Zerleena's gaze lifted from her laptop and turned toward her bedroom. In her mind's eye, she pictured her many shoeboxes full of press clippings of his games, All-Star appearances, and award presentations.

She would burn them after this interview.

"So how are you settling into Brooklyn?" Cornell's question brought her back to his program. "It's different from Miami, right?"

Duh. Zerleena's uncharitable thought grew from

her rising temper. It battled to assert itself over her heartache.

"You can say that again." Marlon's laughter caused her stomach muscles to quiver. She ignored them.

How could her body still react to him this way even after he'd betrayed her a second time? Zerleena clenched her fists. She so badly wanted to be over him.

"I understand we have a mutual acquaintance." Cornell finally came to what Zerleena knew was the reason for this sham interview.

"Are you referring to Zerleena Chase, the *New York Times* best-selling author and host of the award-winning satellite radio show, Zerleena's She Shed? In fact, she just earned her second Best Informational Programming Award Thursday night."

Zerleena frowned. Was Marlon taunting Cornell with her credentials?

"Yes, that's right." Cornell's response was uncertain. His voice was thin. "Zerleena. Do you know why she hates men?"

Here we go. Her salad forgotten, Zerleena pushed away from the table and stood to pace. Through her large, square kitchen window, she absently noted the bluish-gray autumn sky. Fat, white clouds floated past, peering into her condo. How appropriate.

"What makes you think that?" Marlon countered Cornell's inquisition.

Cornell stammered. "Well, for one, the name of her show: Zerleena's *She* Shed? She's deliberately excluding men. And she never has any men on her show. Why not?"

"I have a better question: Why does that bother you?"

Zerleena caught her breath. She spun to face her cell where it lay on her table. All the tension that had been tightening her shoulders and stiffening her back drained at once. Had she been wrong about Marlon's appearance on Cornell's show? She blinked at her phone, hesitant to put her faith in his support. Trust once broken was hard to get back.

Cornell's response was even slower in coming this time. "She's excluding an entire demographic. How's that fair?"

"I don't think that's the real reason you're bothered by Zerleena's show. Come on, buddy. You can tell us." Marlon laughed as though genuinely amused.

Zerleena chuckled in response. An image of Marlon's face as he laughed entered her mind. The curve of his full lips, revealing even, white teeth. The mischievous lights in his midnight eyes. The hard lines of rugged features softening. She used to love to make him laugh. The deep, carefree sound would wrap around her, bringing her joy and filling her heart.

"Of course, that's the reason it bothers me. The *only* reason." Cornell snapped his response.

Zerleena imagined right about now, the satellite radio host was rethinking his eagerness to invite Marlon.

"No, it's not." Marlon was still chuckling.

Zerleena wondered how much of his humor was brought on by Cornell's ridiculous lies and how much was due to his glee in getting under the host's skin. With Marlon, it was hard to tell.

"Oh, yeah? You think you know me so well?" Cornell was becoming belligerent. "Then enlighten me. *You* tell *me* why I'm upset."

"Because she's better than you."

Silence crashed into Cornell's studio. Even Zerleena stopped breathing for a second or two. She hurried back to her table, standing between it and her chair to stare down at her cell, waiting to see — or rather hear — what happened next.

"What?" Cornell's tone rose several octaves. He seemed to be rushing to collect his wits. "That's just crazy."

"No, man, it's a typical baller's trick. When your opponent is as good as you — or in the case of you and Zerleena, better than you — you need an edge. Something to help lift your game above theirs. So you try to get into their head, to take them off their game. The thing is Zerleena knows what you're doing. She's not taking your bait."

"Zerleena Chase isn't better than me." Cornell sounded like he was pushing the words through clenched teeth.

"Yes, she is." Marlon spoke as though his premise had been scientifically proven. Zerleena grinned, unable to believe this was happening. "And when you saw your mind game wasn't working, you decided to invite me to your show to try to double team her. How's that working out for you?"

Zerleena chuckled. "Yes, Corny, how's that working out?"

"This is just crazy." Cornell's voice shook, a sign Marlon had succeeded in rattling him.

"No, crazy is your asserting Zerleena Chase hates anyone." Marlon's words were slow and deliberate. "She doesn't even hate you, although I and a lot of other people wouldn't blame her if she did."

"I haven't—"

Marlon ignored Cornell's interruption. "Zerleena has identified her target audience: women between the ages of twenty-five and fifty-five who want to be financially secure. Your mistake is in thinking that means she's withholding information from other people who might be interested. That's not true. Her program isn't 'No Men Allowed.' It's 'Zerleena's She Shed' and it airs on satellite radio Mondays through Fridays from six AM to eight AM for anyone who wants to listen in."

"Now, wait a minute—"

Marlon talked over Cornell. "Neither her books nor her workshops have exclusionary titles. People can learn more about her books and her workshops on her website."

Zerleena threw back her head and laughed, drowning out the sound of Marlon repeating her website address on the air during Cornell's program. She couldn't buy this kind of positive exposure: A Future

Hall of Fame NBA player, promoting her projects during his interview on her competitor's show.

An epic mic drop.

"Folks, our show will return after this commercial break." Cornell's words were hard and clipped before they were replaced by the jingle of a popular soft drink's ad spot.

Zerleena pressed the computer keys to end Cornell's program. She didn't need to hear anymore.

She threw her arms out and shouted her victory. "Marl, I love you!"

Zerleena froze. Her jaw dropped. Oh, my goodness. She did. She really did. She was in love — still in love — with Marlon Burress. Shaken, she dropped onto the chair behind her.

For the past fifteen years, Zerleena had struggled to get Marlon out of her system. She'd thought she'd been successful. She'd had plenty of other things to focus on: building her career, maintaining her career, growing her career.

Although based on the shoeboxes in her closet and the Miami Waves No. 31 jersey she'd paid the sun and moon for, her efforts had been half-hearted at best. Why hadn't she realized she'd collected shoeboxes full of memorabilia about his college and professional careers, and had shelled out all that money for his jersey because she was still in love with her catastrophe of a college sweetheart? Why had she lied to herself for so long?

And now that she knew, what should she do about

it? Marlon wanted her to let him back into her life. That would be sheer madness.

Wouldn't it?

Zerleena covered her face in her hands, balancing her elbows on her kitchen table. What was she going to do now that he was in New York? Could she trust herself to be "just friends" with her heartbreaker? She couldn't allow Marlon back into her heart. He'd destroy it again. And this time, there wouldn't be any recovering from the devastation.

What should I do?

Her cell phone chimed beside her laptop. D.C. Zerleena sighed before connecting the call.

"Did you hear Burress's interview with Corny?" D.C. didn't wait for Zerleena's greeting.

She made an effort to set aside her concerns and channel enthusiasm into her voice. "Yes, it was great."

"Great?" D.C.'s voice squeaked. "Corny just got *finessed*!" She cackled. "He probably felt liked he'd gone three rounds with a heavyweight. Ha!"

Zerleena laughed. D.C.'s enjoyment swept away most of her fears about Marlon and her heart. "I'm sure he regrets whatever wild hair made him invite Marl to his show."

"No crap. And now he's back from his commercial break and he's gotten rid of Burress." D.C. cackled again.

Zerleena sat back against her seat, taking another few moments to bask in the fact Cornell's plan had gone off the rails. Thanks to Marlon. "That wasn't the interview Corny had planned."

"Hey, you know what? We should invite Burress onto *our* show."

Zerleena's mental brakes screeched to a halt. "We've already talked about this. I'm not going to change my mind." She paced her kitchen again. Her white and silver marbled tiles were smooth and cool beneath her bare feet.

"I know. I know. But your listeners ... they're *really* interested." D.C.'s declaration was punctuated by a buzzer. Her production assistant was eating microwavable lunches again. "We've been getting questions about Burress ever since the *Horn* printed that picture of the two of you on your date, right?"

"Again, that wasn't a date."

"Right. *Not* a date. The two of you just got *all* dressed up and went to a *really* fancy restaurant for dinner and then almost locked lips. But not — *not* — a date."

"Our show isn't all things for all people. We need to stay on brand."

"I think it would be okay to go off brand once in a while to give our listeners what they really want. Within reason." D.C.'s voice faded as though she was moving away from her cell phone.

She was making a good case for her side. Still, Zerleena hesitated. She wasn't anxious for opportunities to see Marlon. Not when her heart was at stake. "What kinds of questions would we allow with this format?"

"You know." D.C.'s response was a verbal shrug meant to mask her eagerness. Zerleena wasn't fooled. "The same kinds of questions they've been calling in with. Like, what's it like playing on his rival's team? How does Brooklyn compare with Miami? Stuff like that."

She sensed a trick. "D.C., we're not going to answer personal questions about me and Marlon."

D.C. exhaled an exasperated breath. "Oh, come on. People *want* to know you better."

"Am I not allowed to have a private life?"

"Sure you are! We just want to know what you do with it."

"I'm serious, D.C. If I open the door to personal questions, the media will kick it down."

D.C. grumbled. "*Fine.* If I promise to screen out the personal questions, will you promise give this idea serious consideration?"

"You can't promise that. Callers snuck in their personal questions last time."

"You can hang up on those."

Zerleena sighed. "Alright. I'll consider it."

She had no doubt D.C. would keep her promise, but what about Marlon? He'd already broken one promise to her since he'd come back into her life. How could she trust him not to break another?

Chapter 9

"You trained him well."

Zerleena had recognized Cornell's number when it showed up on her office phone's caller identification. A call from him at five-thirty in the morning wasn't her ideal way of starting her day, but she'd answered anyway.

She spun her chair to face D.C. She wanted to see her intern's face when D.C. learned who their early morning caller was. "Why are you calling, Cornell?"

D.C. gave her a comical look of surprise. Zerleena swallowed her laughter and waited for Cornell's response.

"How you know Marlon Burress?" He was sulky and still half asleep.

"That's none of your business. And, unlike you, I prepare for my shows so I don't have time to chat."

"And unlike *you*, I don't market myself as an expert on a subject that's so beyond me I need to prepare for my shows."

Zerleena's eyebrows flew up her forehead. She couldn't let that pass. "You host a gossip show that bills itself as a financial consulting program. How was your interview with Marlon Burress supposed to help your listeners manage their finances?"

D.C. swung her arms, whispering urgently. "Leena! *Leena*! Just hang up. Hang up *now*."

Zerleena waved off her friend with her left hand while she gripped her black phone receiver in her right.

Cornell snorted with derision. "Are the two of you in a relationship? I find that hard to believe."

Zerleena stiffened. She was actually offended. "Why? Because you're incapable of interpersonal relationships? Recognizing that's half the battle."

Cornell's laughter was loud, hearty, and forced. "That's rich coming from someone without a personal life."

"You don't know anything about me." Zerleena's hand tightened on the phone. Her body shook with anger, but she kept her voice steady. Will power.

"*Leena*." D.C.'s stage whisper was more frantic. "Hang. Up. *Leena*. Don't let him *goad* you."

Her friend was right, but her advice couldn't penetrate Zerleena's temper.

"I know you're a fraud." The words were almost as mean as his tone. "The only reason you're more successful than me is that you're better at marketing yourself. You're a beautiful woman with a good shtick. People eat that up."

She feared the phone would turn to dust in her vicelike grip. "I'm more successful because I'm better. And that's just killing you."

"How long have you and Marlon Burress been

lovers? Did he bankroll your business? Why are you keeping your relationship secret?"

Zerleena cradled her receiver, resisting the urge to pick it up again and smash it to pieces. It wasn't the phone's fault a rat had been on the other end of the line. "What a pompous—"

Behind her, D.C. tsked. "I *told* you to hang up."

She sent her friend a baleful look before turning away. Sometimes she missed the less assertive D.C. "No one likes to hear, 'I told you so.'"

"Why do you let him goad you? You *know* that's what he wants."

Zerleena bounced her pencil against her desk in an agitated rhythm. "Because it angers me that people like him cash in on favors and connections, then have the nerve, the utter audacity, to claim *I* didn't get here through hard work and merit."

"Why do you care what they think? *You* know the truth so what *they* think shouldn't matter." Wisdom beyond her years.

"But it does." Zerleena sighed, trying and failing to convince her muscles to relax. "It bothers me that I have to work twice as hard, three times as hard, to prove my worth when people like Cornell are given credibility without putting in the effort."

"Leena, your hard work is paying *off*. You know I'm not even gassing you. Just keep doing you and ignore the haters."

Zerleena found a smile. "You're giving me career advice. I thought it was supposed to be the other way around."

D.C.'s brown eyes widened with uncertainty. "I'm—"

"It's good advice. Thank you." Zerleena checked her watch. They had more than an hour before their show. She rose and shrugged into her brown woolen fall jacket. "I need some air."

"'Kay. That's a good idea."

She jogged down the stairs to the lobby and pushed through the office building's front doors. The smell of fresh baked breads and cakes hid just beneath the stench of diesel fuel.

She wove her way into the pedestrian traffic. It was almost six A.M. The sun wasn't up yet, but every Brooklynite seemed to be. How many were starting their day and how many were ending it?

Zerleena buried her hands in her pockets and snuggled further into her coat. The brisk, dew-laden breeze helped clear her head. With her show, manuscript, and workshop, she had too much going on to waste time with Cornell.

But there was one person she wanted to make time for: Marlon. She owed him a proper thank-you. The fact she wanted to deliver it in person didn't have anything to do with her need to see him again — or so she kept telling herself.

***

"You broke your promise to me." Zerleena waited for Marlon just outside the entrance to the Monarchs practice facility late Tuesday afternoon.

She almost laughed at his wide-eyed expression.

His lips parted. He stopped about an arm's length from where she stood several feet from the doorway. "What're you doing here?"

A crisp autumn breeze blew over from the marina, carrying the scent of seawater into the parking lot. The late afternoon sun was just starting to dim, casting longer shadows on the concrete walkway leading from the building's front door to the asphalt parking lot.

Zerleena arched an eyebrow. "Don't try to change the subject. You broke your promise."

He frowned. "What promise?"

"Oh, now that's nice—"

"Excuse me." A deep voice interrupted as Zerleena warmed up her rant.

She shifted her attention to Marlon's right — and froze.

Rick. Evans.

That was *Rick Evans* in front of her. If she only had the courage to stretch out her hand, she could touch the Monarchs' six-foot-six, two-hundred-and-fifteen pound shooting guard. Her mind cleared of everything but Warrick's stats and highlights from the previous season. The professional baller had practically carried the Monarchs through last season's NBA finals and had given her one of the greatest gifts she'd ever received: A title for her beloved hometown professional basketball team.

Unable to speak while so close to one of her sports heroes, Zerleena nodded, encouraging him to continue.

Warrick's half smile was apologetic. "You're Zerleena Chase, aren't you?"

"Yes." Her voice cracked. She cleared her throat and tried again. "Yes, I am. And you're Warrick Evans. Monarchs number 34. Starting shooting guard. Forty-seven percent field goal average. Four-point-one rebound average. Two-point-nine average assists." Zerleena stopped herself before she rambled off additional stats from his previous season's performance. In her peripheral vision, she saw Marlon hook his hands on his hips.

Warrick's expression relaxed with the introductions over. "My wife, Mary, loves your show. She has all of your books."

"Come on, man. Really?" Marlon waved a hand between Warrick and Zerleena.

Warrick chuckled. "Sorry. I had to say something. Mary wouldn't have forgiven me if I hadn't." He turned to leave.

"Wait!" Zerleena hadn't realized she was going to stop him until she did. Her mind went black as he stood waiting for her to speak. "Thank you. And please thank Mary. I'm very flattered."

Grinning, he inclined his head. "I will. And I'm sure she'd want me to say, 'You're welcome.'"

Zerleena sighed as she watched him walk away.

"Earth to Leena. Come in, Leena." Irritation laced Marlon's words. "It's not as though you've never met a baller before."

Zerleena turned her wide-eyed stare to Marlon. She was breathing way too quickly. Her heart was executing mixed martial arts moves in her chest. "*That* was *Rick. Evans.* The man's amazing. And so humble. And he knows who I am! Oh, my gosh! Wait until I tell Key, Erika, and D.C. They're going to flip. Out!"

In her head, Zerleena was having a major meltdown, screaming, and jumping up and down. In real life, a goofy grin felt stapled to her face.

"I know who you are, too." Irritation was still loud and clear in his voice. He crossed his arms over his broad chest.

His black leather jacket was open, revealing his gray sweatshirt. The Miami Waves logo was stitched into the shirt's upper right corner. In deference to Warrick, she wanted to rip the garment from his torso and stomp all over it.

How much longer was he going to wear his former team's fan gear? And why hadn't his teammates stripped it off him and burned it? They probably had other things on their mind, like their losing season.

Zerleena shelved those thoughts for later and returned to their current conflict. "Do you really, Marl? Do you really know who I am?"

"What's that supposed to mean?"

"You broke your promise."

"Leena, I know. And I'm sorry." Marlon placed a hand on the small of her back to guide her into the parking lot. "Let's talk in my car."

Zerleena didn't want to have this conversation in public, either. And although she wasn't angry with Marlon — he'd been masterful during his interview with Cornell — she didn't want him to think he could break his promises to her with impunity. Friends didn't do that.

As he guided her past the black and silver cars in the lot, she strained her neck, twisting it this way and that, hoping to get a glimpse of other Monarchs players.

Across the lot and to her right, Jamal Ward read his cell phone while walking with a scantily clad woman who seemed a few years older than him. Anthony Chambers walked slowly a few strides behind as though praying they wouldn't notice him. To her left, Serge Gateau was folding himself into a black sports sedan. Barron Douglas had parked near him. Neither exchanged a word or even looked at each other. Turning, Zerleena watched Vincent Jardine hurrying from the practice building as though he was late for an appointment.

Five players — six, if you count Warrick — who didn't act like teammates on or off the court. How had they earned a championship ring last season? And how could they even make it to the playoffs this year?

"It's true what people say about the Monarchs not

getting along." Zerleena's shoulders slumped. She didn't know what she'd expected, but this wasn't it.

"What'd you say?" Marlon asked.

She shook her head, turning away from the depressing interactions. "Nothing."

It wasn't hard to locate Marlon's SUV. It was the only vehicle among the fleet of cars in the parking lot that wasn't black, silver, or gray.

He held the passenger side door of his Miami Waves green sedan open for her before circling its hood and settling behind the steering wheel. "I'm sorry, Leena. I really am. My agent thought going on Redd's show would help me connect with local fans."

Zerleena found that strategy questionable. "Does your agent know Corny's show isn't that popular among Monarchs fans?" She watched fascinated as a blush rose into Marlon's cheeks.

"My agent knew Redd wanted to ask me about you. He thought if Redd's listeners knew you and I were friends, it would raise my profile in the market."

Zerleena arched an eyebrow. "Again, the majority of Corny's listeners aren't basketball fans nor are they She Shed fans. I know this because I've done market research. So maybe your agent should leave your publicity to someone else."

Marlon shrugged. "I asked Jett, my agent, to get me on your show, but he said you didn't interview athletes."

"I don't."

Marlon gave her his crooked smile. "I've been listening to your program."

"Oh, yeah?" Zerleena's muscles tightened. Where was Marlon going with this subject change?

"*You* may not want ballers on your show, but your listeners do."

Zerleena smothered a groan. "And there are plenty of sports radio shows for them to listen to."

Marlon inclined his head in silent agreement. "I wasn't going to go on Redd's show. I told Jett the guy was only interested in attacking your reputation. He suggested I use the interview to defend you. So I did."

He had, and Zerleena couldn't be more pleased. But ... "I'm not happy you broke your promise to me. I was pretty clear when I asked you *not* to go on Corny's show. If you were going to change your mind, I wish you'd at least warned me."

"You're right." Marlon sighed his regret. His dark eyes held hers. "I should've given you a head's up. I'm sorry."

Zerleena nodded. "Apology accepted. Don't do it again. Thank you for defending me."

She wasn't sure what had motivated her actions. Impulse pushed her forward. She leaned toward Marlon and pressed her lips to his. It was supposed to be a quick gesture, a small token of appreciation, a brief salutation. But the feel of his lips. The scent of his skin. The heat of his body. So close to hers. They combined, overpowering and overwhelming Zerleena's senses, and clouding her concept of time.

Was she here with him now? Or had they tripped into the past?

Marlon's mouth parted for her. With a moan of yearning — surrender? — Zerleena accepted his invitation. She sent her tongue in search of his. Their reunion was heated, thorough, and long as they explored each other. Zerleena's tongue stroked Marlon's in a new yet familiar caress. Her body trembled and heated in reaction. Her pulse beat a little faster. A little harder.

Zerleena's hands worked their way into his jacket. The play of his broad back muscles beneath her fingertips made her shiver deliciously. The center console pressed into her abdomen. Zerleena ignored it. Marlon deepened their kiss. His mouth was hot, moist, hungry as it explored hers. Zerleena gasped. Her body burned.

She opened her eyes — and remembered where she was. "Marl, wait."

"What?" His voice was low, distracted. He moved his lips lower to her neck. His arms held her closer.

Zerleena shivered in his embrace. She cleared her throat, reluctant to say the words. "We're in the Monarchs parking lot."

Marlon leaned back. Barely. He looked through his windshield. No one was nearby. Yet.

He returned his attention to Zerleena. His hot brown eyes searched her face, feature by feature. "My place?" His invitation was a soft seduction.

"No, Marl." Zerleena moved out of his arms. "I

shouldn't have kissed you. I'm sorry. I gave you the wrong impression."

"I think you're giving me the wrong impression now. I want you, too, Leena." Marlon's voice was as warm and smooth as satin against her skin. He was dangerous.

"Marl, I'm not looking to relive the past."

"Neither am I. I'm asking for a future with you." His deep-voiced declaration went straight to her core. Those words would have meant so much to her fifteen years ago. Today, they filled her with regret. What would they have had together if he'd made a different choice?

Zerleena gritted her teeth against the double allure of his words and those thoughts. The pull was strong. "You don't know me anymore, but you want to build a future with me?"

"I used to know you well, and I'd like to again."

Zerleena rolled her eyes. "That's the other thing, Marlon—"

"I'm back to being 'Marlon.'" He sighed.

"You were always 'Marlon.'" Zerleena adjusted her ruby sweater and the collar of her coffee-colored cotton fall coat as she prepared to get out of the car.

"Well, at least you're saying my name without my having to ask you to."

"The thing is, *Marlon*, you never knew me. If you had, you would've known better than to come looking for me after spending a decade-and-a-half ignoring me." Zerleena reached for the passenger-side door handle.

Marlon leaned over, covering her hand with his. "What're you doing?"

Zerleena looked back. Marlon's chest was pressing against her arm. His soap-and-musk scent surrounded her.

"I'm. Leaving." It was a struggle to sound unaffected by his scent and heat, especially in the suddenly small confines of his spacious SUV.

Marlon carried her hand to his lips. He pressed a kiss to her knuckles then released her. "I'll drive you home."

If he was trying to hypnotize her, it was working. Zerleena gave herself a mental shake. "I can take the train. That' show I got here." Her voice sounded weird. It was his fault.

"Please, Leena. I'll take you straight home. Promise." Marlon put his hand on her knee. The warmth from his touch traveled up her thigh.

"Straight home." Zerleena removed his hand. "And no touching."

"You have my word." Marlon's smile was relieved as he guided his car out of the parking lot and into the late afternoon traffic. "Do you have a car?"

"Why are you asking? Do you think my feelings toward you will warm up if you buy me one?" Zerleena squeezed her eyes shut and pressed her lips together. Every snippy word from her lips revealed how much he affected her. She had to stop sabotaging herself.

Marlon sent her a quick, confused glance. "I was just curious."

Her cheeks heated. "I'm sorry I snapped at you."

He grinned at the windshield. "Based on what I've read about you on the internet, I should be asking *you* to buy *me* a car."

She surprised herself with a laugh. "It's because I don't buy cars for other people that I've been able to build on my savings."

"Thanks for the tip." The sound of Marlon's laughter strummed the muscles in her abdomen.

She shifted on her seat. There was a time when his laughter filled her with joy. Today, it was making her restless. "I have a car, but I rarely drive in the city. It's more for traveling. I have a driver or use the subway."

Zerleena forced herself to ignore the way Marlon's warmth seemed to embrace her inside his car. The bumper-to-bumper traffic gave her more time to people watch through the passenger-side window. The sidewalks were teaming with pedestrians strolling, shopping, or rushing back to work.

She guided their conversation to more casual topics: weather, traffic, upcoming holidays, and favorite landmarks. Thankfully, it wasn't long before Marlon pulled up in front of her condo building.

She reached for the door handle before he brought the car to a standstill. "Thanks again for the lift."

His voice stopped her. "Would you like to have dinner?"

Zerleena froze with her back to him. Her body

would love to have dinner with Marlon, but her mind was dead set against it. It took an effort to turn him down. "I don't think that would be a good idea. I don't want to blur the boundaries of our friendship."

"Friends have dinner together all the time." He deliberately misunderstood her concern. She was sure of it.

"It wouldn't be a good idea at least not now." Zerleena faced him, holding his gaze. "Maybe it's me. Maybe I'm the only one having trouble with our boundaries."

"If that's the boundary you want to set, then I have to respect it. I don't want to lose your friendship." Marlon gave her a quizzical smile. "If dinner's out at least for now, how about tickets to tomorrow's game?"

"I—" Zerleena was about to say she had tickets to the Monarchs. Then she remembered she'd told Marlon she didn't follow professional basketball any longer. She caught herself just in time. She wasn't ready to admit she hadn't been entirely truthful about that. "No, thank you."

Marlon inclined his head. His smile faded slightly as though her decline disappointed him. "Are you sure? Attending a live Monarchs game might reawaken your fandom."

Zerleena smiled as she shook her head. "I don't think so."

"Okay, but let me know if you change your mind."

"I will." Zerleena started to climb out of his car.

"And, Leena."

She paused, finding him over her shoulder. "What is it?"

"Let me know if you change your mind about my being on your show, too."

"Thanks, Marl." She sang her response in mock exaggeration.

Some of the glow returned to his smile at the sound of his nickname from her lips. "Any time."

Zerleena stepped back from the curb to watch him drive off. His taillights quickly vanished into traffic.

Friendship. With Marlon Burress. It wasn't one of my smarter ideas.

She shook her head as she entered her building. Zerleena tossed the security guards a distracted smile on her way to the elevator banks. She had to keep tugging her thoughts from the spontaneous kiss she and Marlon had shared.

What had gotten into her? Kissing Marlon Burress was a mistake she couldn't afford. For the sake of her heart and mind, she had to keep her distance from him — regardless of what her body wanted.

Chapter 10

"Look who I met on my way into your building." Zerleena's father's smile rivaled the sun as he stood in her doorway. Ramone jerked his head toward his left shoulder, as though she could miss Marlon behind him. "I realized right away he must be on his way to see you just as I was, so I let the guard on duty know he was with me."

"That's wonderful. Thanks, Dad." Keeping her smile in place, Zerleena let both men into her home.

Ramone crossed her threshold, carrying the box of presentation materials she'd loaned her mother for a block association's meeting earlier in the week.

She caught Marlon's scent as he past her. Her heart bounced in a way that irritated her. It had been almost a month since she'd last seen him. He'd been driving away from the curb outside of her building. Since then, Thanksgiving had come and gone. The Monarchs had lost three of their last four games, extending their record to 6-15. Fortunately, they were off today and tomorrow, but would those forty-eight hours be enough to get their act together? She doubted it.

Setting aside her concern for her team, Zerleena concentrated on getting through Marlon's surprise appearance during her father's visit. Her eyes wanted to eat him up. He was a visual treat in narrow-legged dark blue jeans. His sage leather winter coat was unzipped, showcasing a navy knit sweater that molded his lean torso.

"Your father and I had a very interesting conversation in the elevator." Marlon's voice rolled with humor as he faced her in the archway that led to her living room.

"Oh? About what?" She tried to read the reason for Marlon's amusement in his expression.

Ramone grunted. "For some reason, Marl had the crazy idea you don't follow basketball anymore. Can you believe it?"

Zerleena's wide-eyed gaze shot to Marlon's laughing brown eyes. "Really?" She croaked the question.

Ramone shook his head as he continued into Zerleena's living room. "He thought you didn't support the Monarchs anymore. Isn't that crazy?"

Zerleena cleared her throat. She pulled her eyes from Marlon's mockery and hurried after her father. "Yeah. Crazy. Weird. Right?"

"Your father was *stunned* at the idea." Marlon's response sounded choked as though he was forcing back laughter.

Zerleena hummed. "Oh, yeah. I could imagine."

Marlon continued. "I wonder what — or *who* — would've given me such a preposterous and weirdly inaccurate idea."

Zerleena avoided his gaze as though her life depended on it. She searched her mind for some kind of response that would get her out of this situation.

Thankfully, Marlon didn't seem to expect an answer. "Fortunately, your father set me straight."

Zerleena shot a quick glance at him over her shoulder. "Well. That's good."

Marlon closed the distance between them. "Yes. He told me you have all the Monarchs gear: clothing, accessories, houseware. He said you even get season tickets to every home game every year, including this year. Imagine that."

"Imagine." Zerleena's voice was weak. She turned toward her father. "Dad, thank you for bringing back all of this stuff. You didn't have to. I would've gotten them when I came for dinner."

Ramone waved her off. "It wasn't a problem." With his hands now free, he wrapped her in a warm hug and kissed the top of her head. "But I'd better get going. I told your mother I'd pick up a few things from the store on my way home."

Zerleena stepped back from his embrace. Should she ask her father to stay? He could be a buffer between her and Marlon, especially since Marlon now knew she'd lied to him about her disinterest in the NBA. His arched eyebrow warned of a heck of an interrogation in her very near future. Good grief.

On second thought, it would be better for her to handle this alone. She straightened her spine and escorted her father to her door. "Give Mom my love."

"I will." Ramone nodded at Marlon. "It's good to see you again, and great to have you with the Monarchs."

"Thank you, sir." Marlon smiled.

"And don't worry about this rough patch. We have sixty-one more games. We'll turn it around."

A cloud crossed Marlon's face before he steadied his smile. "I hope so, too, sir. Thank you."

After showing her father out, Zerleena took a moment to compose herself.

"You're still a basketball fan." Marlon's amused words carried from behind her.

She faced him. He still stood just in front of her living room. He hadn't removed his coat. His arms hung at his sides.

She shrugged. "I admit I enjoyed rooting against the Waves when you played the Monarchs."

"Does that mean you rooted *for* us when we played everyone else?"

Zerleena's lips curved into a reluctant smile. She shook her head. "What an ego."

"You only have yourself to blame." He sobered. "Why'd you tell me you'd stopped watching the NBA?" Marlon didn't seem angry or impatient. His expression was curious.

"I don't know." Zerleena's words came out on a sigh.

Marlon's eyebrows knitted. "You don't know why you lied to me?"

Zerleena flinched. When put that way, her sins

seemed to be compounded. "I do know, but I don't want to tell you."

A flicker of a smile sparkled in his dark eyes. "Tell me anyway. I really want to know."

Zerleena lifted her chin in defiance. "I told you I no longer followed professional basketball because..." She stumbled, then strengthened her resolve. "Because you hurt me. There. I said it. I didn't want to admit you and I had anything in common anymore. Or that I've seen you play in the pros, even inadvertently, when the Waves played the Monarchs."

Marlon looked wounded and concerned. He crossed her hallway in two large strides. His gaze compelled her to look at him. "Leena, I'm so sorry for the hurt I caused you. I know I could never apologize enough but I *am* sorry. I've made some stupid, stupid mistakes in my life—"

"Yes, you have."

"My media image as a conceited baller. Wasting money on stupid stuff like a boat I can't even sail." He smiled at Zerleena's startled laughter. "I should have asked you to manage my money." He grew serious again. "But by far the dumbest thing I've ever done was leaving you."

Zerleena caught her breath. She'd be lying to herself this time if she pretended she hadn't fantasized about receiving some version of those words from this man. On the contrary, she'd had that dream several times a year before finally picking up the pieces of her heart and trying to move on. Yet after all these years, when she'd thought she was beginning to get over him, Marlon Burress sauntered back into her life and helped her live out her fantasy.

What am I supposed to do now?

Zerleena circled him to walk on shaky legs into her living room. She wasn't running away. She just needed space to think. Or so she told herself. "OK. Well. Thank you for saying that. Is there anything else?"

Marlon had followed her. "Leena." He sighed her name, making her toes curl inside her fuzzy silver socks. "I know we agreed to just be friends, but you know I want another chance for us. I've never gotten over you, Leena."

She threw out her arms. "Now you're making me mad."

He frowned. "Why?"

"I don't believe a word of what you've said. Not one word."

"It's the truth."

"Ha!" She forced a loud, mocking bark of laughter. "You never got over me? Then why didn't you try to contact me? You've had *fifteen*. Years." Zerleena spun on her heels to pace toward her large picture window. "Why didn't you know what I've been doing? You wouldn't have had to friend me on social media or subscribe to my enewsletter. You could've found out with a simple internet search, but you didn't even do that. So explain, if you never got over me, how were you able to keep me so far out of your mind?"

Marlon walked toward her. "You're right. I didn't do an internet search on you. But I couldn't avoid updates about you in our alumni newsletter. I never got over you, but I tried. I thought it would be easier to move on if I didn't dwell on you, but it's not." He stopped in front of her, blocking her from pacing or otherwise getting away from him.

"Maybe you should try harder." She attempted to shove past him but he wouldn't budge.

"Here's what I do know about the present Leena Chase. You helped establish an organization that encourages girls to pursue careers in financial investment. You helped establish a program that provides college scholarships for homeless women. And I know that, of all your accomplishments, you're most proud of those."

Zerleena crossed the room and dropped onto the sofa. "I've never publically spoken about my connection to those organizations. How did you know about them?"

The only people she'd discussed those with were Erika and Keysha, who were partners in those ventures with her, and her parents.

"I'm one of your many anonymous donors. I have been from the start." Marlon sat beside her. "When your fund-raisers solicit donations, they mention you among their founding members."

"I had no idea you were a donor." She didn't realize she'd whispered the words aloud until he smiled.

Marlon shifted closer to her. "I know I was a grade

A jerk to you, Leena. I know I don't deserve a second chance, but I'm asking — pleading — for one anyway."

Her head was spinning. Speechless, she returned his gaze. Marlon's eyes were clear and vulnerable as they searched hers. Her heart melted under their intensity.

It was as though he'd read her mind and was acting out her secret fantasy. Yes, he'd been cavalier with her heart in their past. For that, she'd wanted to hurt him even more than she'd needed to protect herself. Now he was asking for forgiveness and a second chance. In her daydreams, she'd always laughed in his face and turned him away. Payback had seemed so sweet. Faced with her fantasy come to life, she made a game time decision to go with a different play.

Without conscious thought, she'd moved closer to him. She cupped the side of his face. His skin was warm beneath her palm. She drew him to her as she parted her lips. Marlon covered her mouth with his. She sighed into his kiss. She'd missed this so much. Their previous kiss in his car had been a tease and a taunt, reminding her of their past. In Marlon's arms today, she sensed he was focused on their present and wanted to share a taste of what their future could be. His lips and tongue explored every inch of hers, meeting her needs yet leaving her wanting so much more.

Zerleena slid her hands beneath his coat and over his torso. She paused at his well-developed pecs. His muscles heated her palms. Her hands moved back down, stopping at his waist to slip under his sweater.

His abdominals quivered as her palms moved over them.

Marlon groaned deep in his throat. He pulled her closer to him, pinning her hands between them. He raised his head, freeing her mouth. His eyes burned into hers. "If this isn't what you want, tell me now and I'll leave."

"Do you have a condom?" Zerleena's skin tingled and her mouth watered as her palms traced his tight, hard muscles.

"Yes."

Ding! Ding! Ding! Right answer!

But... Zerleena gave him a suspicious look. "Egotistical?"

Marlon shrugged his eyebrows. "Hopeful."

"Then, yes, this is what I want."

With a smile, part pleasure, part relief, Marlon shook off his coat. He grabbed the hem of his sweater with his right hand and stripped it off. Her breath caught in her throat. Time had loved him well. The lean, wiry strength of his youth had grown into the mature, well-developed sculpture of the man.

Her eyes ate every inch of his exposed skin. Pressing those muscles against her had stirred a yearning. Tracing them had sparked a desire. Now seeing them exposed before her was pouring gasoline on a barbecue. Her hunger wouldn't, couldn't be denied.

Zerleena stood with Marlon. She lifted up on her toes as she brought his head to hers for another, deeper kiss. She walked him backward to her bedroom, discarding clothing — his and hers — along the way.

By the time they'd reach the foot of her bed, they'd stripped to their underwear. Marlon stepped back and Zerleena's pale indigo bra dropped to her bedroom's hardwood flooring. The hunger in his eyes caused her nipples to tighten. With a gentle shove to his shoulders, she toppled him onto her bed.

For a moment, she watched him lying in the middle of her queen-sized mattress, wearing only his smoke gray boxers. He looked like an ad for pleasant dreams.

Zerleena rescued his black leather wallet from his brown dockers and tossed it to him. "Is it in there?"

Marlon placed his condom beside him on the abstract patterned black-silver-and-gray comforter, and tossed his wallet aside. "Come get it." His voice was a husky invitation.

Zerleena didn't need a second summons. She stripped off her tan cotton underwear and straddled Marlon's lean hips. The feel of his hard hot body between her naked thighs caused their past and present to collide. Marlon was broader than he'd been in college. His muscles even more clearly defined. And in his eyes, there was an awareness of her she'd never seen before; a focus on her that caused the muscles in her abdomen to tremble and the heat at the juncture of her thighs to intensify.

She took hold of the waistband of his boxers and pulled them past his lean hips, powerful thighs, and strong calves. Zerleena let the garment drop to the floor. She made her way back up his body, pausing to stroke her tongue along the length of his impressive erection. Zerleena heard his groan, watched his muscles flex, and felt her body moisten.

Their combined body heat should have scorched her bedding. He wrapped her in his arms, holding her closer, tighter until she couldn't distinguish his heartbeat from hers. She pressed against him, burying her face in his neck. The scent of his desire clouded her mind and fueled her hunger. They rolled across her mattress as they explored each other. They rediscovered each other's pleasure points with kisses, nibbles, and touches.

Zerleena burned. She pressed her hands against Marlon's chest. Pressing him over, she straddled him.

"Playtime's over." Her words were low and raspy as though they came from someone else's voice.

She dug through the tangled comforter for the condom packet, growing more impatient with each passing nanosecond. Finally, she recovered it. Ripping the packet open, she rolled the protection onto him.

"Leena." Marlon's voice was choked.

He was hard. He was hot. And she was ready. So ready. She shifted over him, welcoming him inside her. Her breath caught as he filled her. Her body shivered as he warmed her.

Zerleena arched her back, finding their half-forgotten but well-remembered rhythm in a far corner of her mind. She closed her eyes with a sigh.

"Oh, Marl." She pressed her lips together against the rest of that thought, *I've missed you so much.*

"I know, baby." He answered as though he'd read her mind. "I missed you, too."

Marlon gripped her thighs as he caught her rhythm, pushing against her, into her. Zerleena's muscles squeezed him. Marlon's fingers grazed her inner thighs, inching higher. Slowly. Zerleena held her breath. But Marlon's hands, changed direction, wrapping around her waist.

She groaned. "Don't stop."

"I won't." His voice was hypnotic.

Was this a dream?

Zerleena's eyes popped open. She placed her right hand over Marlon's heart. It pounded against her palm.

Not a dream. So real.

With his hands against her back, Marlon drew Zerleena to him. His lips closed around her nipple, suckling her, licking her, teasing her.

Zerleena closed her eyes again, almost overwhelmed by the dual points of pleasure. Her hips rocked faster. She gritted her teeth as the sharp sweetness rolled over her. Marlon's hands moved down her back to cup her hips. He urged her on, pressing her tighter. Holding her closer.

And then he touched her. There.

Her muscles drew tighter and tighter and tighter. Her body convulsed as she exploded over him. Marlon stiffened between her thighs. His body arched, lifting her. She lost her breath, then found it. Zerleena collapsed onto Marlon. He rolled with her onto his side and tucked her into him.

***

"You've got to be kidding." Marlon's voice carried over from the pillow beside hers. His hot, hard body was spooned around her.

Zerleena slapped her alarm clock, shutting off the obnoxious noise. She turned over without dislodging the arm Marlon had wrapped around her waist. Usually, she jumped out of bed, ready and rearing to start her day. But this morning, with his body warming hers and his scent surrounding her, she wanted to linger.

She curled into him. His chest hair tickled her nose as she breathed him in. Her body pulsed as he drew her closer. "When I invited you to stay the night, I warned you I set my alarm for three-fifteen." For the first time in years, she resented her schedule.

"Three-fifteen didn't sound as bad in the abstract. It's the reality I'm having trouble with." Marlon groaned as he drew her closer to him. "Besides you wore me out last night. I didn't have the energy to leave."

"This from an elite athlete with two championship rings and an MVP trophy. Give me a break." Zerleena planted a quick kiss on the center of his chest before regretfully tearing herself from him. He felt so good and smelled so fine.

A cold draft caught her as she tossed back the comforter, blanket and sheet. Talk about reality slapping you in the face. Zerleena stood and stretched. The cotton nightgown she'd changed into after she and Marlon had eaten dinner and gone back to bed floated around her. It was a poor substitute for his arms.

Marlon climbed out of bed from the other side. "Damn, it's cold."

She grinned as she switched on the lamp on her nightstand. "December mornings in Brooklyn. Don't worry. Your Sunshine State blood will toughen up after one good winter."

She turned to face him. His naked body scrambled her thoughts. Her eyes traced the path from his sculpted chest, six-pack abs, and narrow hips to his long, powerful legs. Zerleena followed his flexing muscles as Marlon circled her bed.

"It's not the winter I'm worried about. It's right now." He scooped her into his arms and turned toward her bathroom. His smile was suggestive. "Maybe a hot shower to warm us up."

A little more than an hour later, Marlon dropped Zerleena off at work. The lift kept her from being late. As it was, she had only minutes to spare before her five AM start time for her six AM show. But Marlon's driving her to work also gave her the unsettling sense of their being a couple. Was that what they were after last night?

Marlon shifted the gear into park, then searched

her face. His smile was easy but his eyes were guarded. Was he as nervous as she was? She hoped so.

"Why don't I make us dinner tonight?"

Zerleena's eyebrows leaped up her forehead. Amusement nudged out discomfort. "I don't know about that, Marl. I remember your previous attempt to cook dinner for me. It didn't turn out so well."

Marlon laughed without remorse. "That was our senior year. The pot roast got the best of me."

"You gave me food poisoning."

Surprise stamped his expression. "No, I didn't."

"You came close."

"But I didn't make you sick. And I promise I've had a lot of practice cooking for myself over the years. You'll be perfectly safe."

"Well, since I'm feeling adventurous, I'll accept your invitation. Thank you."

"Great. I'll pick you up at your place at five o'clock."

"It's a date." Zerleena froze, suddenly fearful. What had last night been, a farewell to their past? A welcome to a new beginning? Both? Was she fooling herself? Again?

"A real date this time." Marlon's eyes darkened. He pressed his lips to hers. His kiss was a sweet promise that Zerleena wanted to trust.

"Have a good practice." She hurried from Marlon's car without waiting to hear his response.

Before slipping into her studio building, she glanced back at the street. Marlon was still parked at the curb. It was too dark to tell whether he was watching her. Just in case, she lifted a hand in a brief farewell, then rushed inside.

Last night, he'd made so many of her fantasies come true, but she still remembered how much their breakup had hurt. Did she want to give him that much power over her? Again?

Chapter 11

He'd made them salmon, asparagus spears, gluten-free dinner rolls, and a spring mix garden salad. Marlon was confident in his cooking abilities. He'd been honest when he'd told Zerleena he preferred to cook. It was better than going out all the time, especially since he was recognizable.

Then why was he on the verge of passing out as he waited for her reaction to their meal?

Zerleena sampled the salmon. Her brown eyes lit up and her lips curved into an appreciative smile. "This is fantastic."

His shoulder muscles relaxed. "Told you so."

Zerleena threw her head back and laughed. "You were nervous. Admit it. I thought I'd have to give you CPR."

"What made you think that?" Marlon couldn't meet her eyes as he battled back a smile.

"Because you were staring at me like this." Zerleena mimicked him with an exaggerated wide-eyed stare before dissolving into peals of laughter again. "Admit it. Admit it."

"OK." Marlon gave her his crooked smile. He drew a breath, filling his senses with the buttery aromas of their dinner. "I may have been a little nervous. That Pot Roast Meal of Shame scarred me."

"You? I was the one with food poisoning."

"It was *not* food poisoning. Will you stop saying that?"

Zerleena masked her mocking smile by taking a sip of ice tea.

Marlon rolled his eyes. "Anyway, I was determined to make a better impression this time."

"You have." Zerleena returned to her dinner. "This meal is wonderful. Thank you."

"Thank *you*." Marlon settled back against his chair.

Their conversation drifted to more impersonal topics: events from their day, autumn and winter in Brooklyn, books, movies, and music.

Marlon noticed Zerleena's curious gaze roaming his dining room. What did she think about his decorating skills? Should he hang more pictures in his dining room? The plain white walls looked a little bare. And his glass-and-wood, rectangular dining table could use a centerpiece. He hadn't thought of that in his panic to make the perfect meal.

From her seat across the table from him, Marlon knew Zerleena could see past his kitchen into his living room. He brought an image of the room to mind. Perhaps he could have put more of an effort into arranging the mismatched framed photographs and odd little knickknacks that lined up across his Maplewood fireplace mantel. He'd bought his overstuffed teal sofa, loveseat, and armchair first and foremost for comfort. Anxious for her approval, he searched her face for even a hint of her reaction. He wanted her to feel comfortable and enjoy spending time in his home.

"How are things going with the team?" Zerleena finished her iced tea. "You told me you were having trouble winning over the locker room."

Marlon sighed as he refilled her glass from the pitcher between them. He'd hoped to keep their conversation light. That wouldn't be possible if the discussion shifted to the team. "Unfortunately, nothing's changed. They still haven't accepted me."

"Why do you think that is?" She nodded her thanks for her refill, then nudged aside her plate and silverware. Marlon had used what his mother would call his good dishes.

He shrugged. "The Monarchs and the Waves have always been rivals. No Monarch has ever played for the Waves and, to my knowledge, I'm the only Waves player ever to be traded to the Monarchs."

"So you think it's a culture clash?"

Something in her voice alerted Marlon that Zerleena may have a different theory. "I think that's part of it. What d'you think?"

Her attention once again drifted over his shoulder toward his living room before returning to him. "I think the Monarchs realize you don't want to be here."

Marlon stiffened. He struggled to keep from sounding defensive. "What makes you think that?"

"It's just a hunch, mind you, but the players have

probably noticed you're still wearing a lot of your Waves fan gear."

"What does it matter what I wear when I'm not working?" Marlon stood to clear the table. "I wear my Monarchs uniform on the court."

Zerleena's eyes sparkled with humor as she collected her place setting and rose from the table. "It obviously matters to *you* otherwise you wouldn't wear your *Waves* jerseys, sweatshirts, and warmup pants to the *Monarchs* practice facility."

Marlon's attention dropped to the dishes in Zerleena's arms. "You don't need to clear the table. You're my guest."

Zerleena gave him a saucy look as she walked past him into his kitchen. "We're beyond being each other's 'guest,' aren't we?"

Marlon grinned and followed her. "So you think the Monarchs are freezing me out because of my T-shirts?"

"You're treating this like a joke." She deposited her place setting in his dishwasher, then stepped back to give him access. "Think about the situation in reverse. Imagine instead of *you* being traded to the Monarchs, Rick Evans was traded to the Waves and you were still in Miami."

"What's this obsession you have with Evans?" He hadn't intended the question to sound so gruff.

She ignored him. "What would you think if Rick came to every practice in Monarchs gear?"

Marlon paused with his hand on the glass he'd

loaded into the dishwasher. His face heated from his visceral reaction to the imaginary insult, but also with embarrassment. "I hadn't thought about that." He straightened and faced her. "That would get under my skin."

"That's what you're doing to your teammates every time you walk into *their* practice facility, wearing their *division rival's* logo."

He sighed. "I get it. It's more than just a jersey. And it doesn't matter that I change out of it as soon as I get to the locker room. It's the fact I'm wearing it at all that's probably bothering them."

"There's no *probably* about it."

"You're right."

"Which brings me to another point."

Marlon's neck and shoulder muscles tightened. "There's more?"

"Why do you keep referring to your team as 'the Monarchs'?"

He frowned. "What am I supposed to call them?"

"'Us' or 'we.'" Zerleena knitted her eyebrows. "You're a Monarch, too. In this version of us-versus-them, your 'us' is the Monarchs. The Waves are now the 'them.'"

Marlon massaged the back of his neck. "Why were you able to see this and I couldn't?"

Zerleena reached out, taking his left hand. Her smile was kind, easing his embarrassment by forgiving him for his oversight. "You're not known for being self-aware."

"So I've been told." Marlon entwined his fingers with hers.

Zerleena smiled up into his face. "As a Monarchs fan, seeing you in Miami Waves gear gets under my skin. I can only imagine how much more irritating it is for the team."

It wasn't just the team. It was the entire franchise. He remembered a question Troy Marshall, the Monarchs marketing executive, had asked after a practice, *"Do you need help finding Monarchs gear?"*

How could he have missed that?

He and DeMarcus had played together for the Waves. DeMarcus had spent his entire career with the Miami team, something Marlon had expected to do also.

"Thank you for making me understand that." Marlon carried Zerleena's hand to his lips. "I guess I have some online shopping to do tomorrow."

"Tomorrow?" Zerleena stepped closer to him. She lowered her voice. "Are you so very busy tonight?"

Marlon's body responded to the heat in Zerleena's gaze and the suggestion in her tone.

"I hope to be." He lowered his head to capture her lips with his.

***

Why did he feel like he'd been called to the principal's office? Marlon tapped twice on Jaclyn Jones's office door. "Coach said you wanted to speak with me." He was tempted to add, *Principal Jones.*

Jaclyn's assessing cinnamon gaze pinned him to the threshold for just a moment before her features eased into a welcoming smile. "Thank you for your time, Marl. Please make yourself comfortable." Her honey-and-whiskey voice welcomed him as she gestured toward the three black cushioned visitors' chairs in front of her large mahogany desk.

Crossing into the office, Marlon caught the scent of strong coffee and Jaclyn's soft feminine fragrance.

He settled onto the closest chair and propped his right ankle on his left knee. His gaze swept the Monarchs owner's/general manager's office, taking in the thick silver carpet, comfortable black furniture, and bright white walls. Her scarlet jacket and matching fingernail polish provided the only color in the room. Her fitted jacket highlighted the rose undertone of her golden brown skin. Her thick, curly brown hair was swept behind her narrow shoulders. Jaclyn Jones was a beautiful and brilliant woman. Marlon had a great deal of respect for her.

During her successful career in the Women's National Basketball Association, the media had referred to the former shooting guard as the Lady Assassin. The title was a reflection of her holding the fewest number of fouls while claiming one of the highest scoring records in the league.

The past few seasons hadn't been easy for Jaclyn. After the death of her grandfather, one of the team's founders, she'd been committed to preserving his legacy. That meant wrestling control of the franchise from her business partners, one of whom had been infuriatingly disinterested in the team and the other had been a scheming fraud.

It had taken courage, confidence, and an impressive strategy to gain control of the franchise and turn it from being the worst team in the league to the season's NBA champion. Part of her strategy had involved recognizing DeMarcus was the head coach she needed to turn her chronically losing team into winners.

Marlon turned his attention back to Jaclyn and found her watching him as intently as he'd studied her office. It was a struggle not to squirm under her steady, enigmatic stare.

"There are rumors around the league you're shopping for a trade." Jaclyn held his gaze as she spoke.

He'd worried she'd learn about his agent's efforts to get him out of Brooklyn. But his desire to find a better professional situation for himself was stronger than his concern about insulting his boss. He wasn't going to let fear prevent him from pursuing a more suitable deal.

Marlon spread his hands. "I don't know what's going to happen at the end of the season."

Jaclyn's perfectly arched eyebrows knitted. "The season's barely started. We've played just twenty-three games."

And the Monarchs — we — have lost seventeen of

them. This isn't the way he'd imagined ending his career.

Marlon dragged his thoughts away from that cliff. "You've only signed me to a one-year contract. I can't wait until the season's over to decide what I'm going to do next. This isn't a date. It's my life."

"I understand." Jaclyn settled back against her black faux leather executive chair. Her eyes remained watchful. "I also know you have more control over this situation than you think. *This* contract is for a year, but I was hoping you'd want to be with the team beyond that."

Marlon cocked his head. "Then why did you sign me to one season?"

"I want you on our team." Jaclyn spoke faster. "Your game qualities complement the skill sets we already have and that'll make us stronger. You've mastered not only the physical skills but the mental game."

"Thank you." Marlon searched Jaclyn's expression. What was she saying?

She continued as though he hadn't spoken. "Other teams are drafting and trading for younger players. They think they'll win by filling their rosters with speed and energy. Sure, they'll have the physicality, but it'll take them years to get the mentality. With you, Rick, and Vinny, we'll always have that strategic edge on the court. We won't have to outplay them. We'll outwit them. They may have youth and beauty, but we'll have brains and experience."

"And beauty."

"Of course." Jaclyn's eyes sparkled as though she thought he was teasing. He wasn't.

A weight dropped from Marlon's shoulders. "This is the first time anyone's pointed out the positives of my age."

"Age doesn't necessarily bring wisdom." Jaclyn waved a dismissive hand. "There are plenty of ballers your age and older who still don't get it. You, Rick, and Vinny are not only students of the game; you can read people. You can use their weaknesses as well as their strengths against them."

Marlon tried to use that discernment on Jaclyn. His boss wasn't giving him much to work with. Her expression was neutral. Her body language was relaxed. Her tone was enthusiastic, but Marlon was suspicious. "This all sounds very nice."

Jaclyn tossed him a grin. "It does, doesn't it? I'm excited about this strategy."

And he was baffled. "But you haven't explained why you only offered a one-year contract?"

"On paper, you're a good match for the team. But I have concerns about the chemistry." She gave him a direct look. "I won't sacrifice the locker room for you, Marl."

Marlon understood her approach. As exciting as her plans for the franchise's future were, they wouldn't work if the team couldn't come together. Right now, the team's unity was in serious doubt. "How d'you think I'm fitting in?"

Jaclyn arched an eyebrow, evading his question. "How do *you* think you're fitting in?"

"We both know I'm not." Although things had gotten better once he'd stopped wearing his Waves gear to the practice facility. "We also both know I'm not the only problem in the locker room."

"You're right." Jaclyn's sigh carried a wealth of irritation. Her attention drifted from him to a corner of her office. Was she picturing their heart-breaking one-point loss to the Indiana Pacers at home Sunday night? "I thought the championship had cured that. Instead they brought all of their old resentments and jealousies with them to our new season."

"It seems that way." Marlon shook his head. "So am I one-and-done?"

Jaclyn's gaze returned to him. Her focus sharpened. "There are fifty-nine games left to the season. You tell me. Are you calling it quits already?"

Marlon tensed at the idea of quitting. He stood. "I may be a lot of things, Jackie, but I'm not a quitter."

"I'm glad to hear it."

He held her gaze, reading the silent challenge in her eyes. *Prove it.*

Without responding, Marlon strode from the room. He wasn't quitting on the Monarchs. They were the ones who'd closed the door on him before the season had started. If he wanted to stay on the team, he needed a plan to force it open.

Chapter 12

"Come on already. Tell me what we're celebrating." Zerleena made her demand from the other side of their cozy booth table at the West Indian restaurant in downtown Brooklyn.

She'd suggested the family-style establishment. The young host had greeted her like a blood relative — or an investor. Marlon had been aware of the eager stares and excited whispers that had tracked them to this relatively secluded section of the dining area. He'd been under no illusions the attention had been meant for him. For the first time in his fifteen-year career, he wasn't the center of attention while out in public — and he didn't mind. In fact, he was proud of the reaction she was drawing.

Marlon smiled at her expression. Her dark eyes shone like diamonds in her excitement. "Don't you want to order first?"

Zerleena issued a warning look. "I already know what I'm getting, curried chicken. It comes with rice and peas, fried plantain, and a side salad."

"That sounds good. I'll have the same." Marlon closed his menu and swung his gaze around the restaurant.

The atmosphere was warm and friendly. Strong,

bright reds, greens, and golds dominated the décor. Animated conversations and bursts of laughter carried from other tables. The air was swollen with the scents of curry, peppers, and meats. Reggae fusion played in the background. It was loud enough to encourage chair dancing, but soft enough not to impede private conversations.

"Alright, then. Spill it."

Marlon brought his attention back to Zerleena. Her appearance was another reason they were drawing so much attention from fellow diners. She was beautiful in an emerald green sweater dress that skimmed her slender, well-toned figure. The knee-high split had given him flirty glimpses of her right calf as he'd followed her to their table. She'd accessorized her outfit with chunky bronze earrings.

Marlon battled back a grin. "So this is what it feels like to date a celebrity."

She raised a winged eyebrow. "Have you really so quickly forgotten the models and singers you've dated over the years?"

Marlon searched her expression for jealousy or resentment. All he found was amusement curving her full lips. "I may have gone out a few times with a couple of models and singers, but they weren't as well-known in the local community as you are. And we weren't dating."

"Oh, come on." Zerleena's surprised laughter mocked him. "Aren't you splitting hairs? What's the difference between *dating* and *going out*?"

Their server arrived, introducing himself then taking their entrée requests. Marlon waited until the young man collected their menus and stepped away. "The difference is *going out* isn't serious. *Dating* is."

Her eyes still sparkled with humor. "And who decides whether it's *going out* or *dating*?"

"It's a mutual decision."

"I don't know, Marl. They sound like the same thing."

"They're not. For example, we're dating."

The twinkle in her eyes flickered and faded. "Are you suggesting we're in a serious relationship?"

"Are you suggesting we're not?"

Her eyes wavered before her expression closed. It was as though she'd drawn a curtain between them. She sat back against the cushioned bench seating. "What're we celebrating?"

Marlon noticed the lack of inflection in her voice. He could feel her tension across the table. Should he follow her play and change the subject or press for an answer to his question? He'd let her make the call, if only to keep the peace. For now. "I spoke with Jackie Jones today. She's willing to extend my contract, if I'm interested in staying with the Monarchs."

Zerleena searched his face as though trying to read his thoughts. Meanwhile her expression kept him out of hers. "And are you interested?"

He'd hoped for a more enthusiastic reaction. Was she still judging him by the boneheaded mistakes of his youth? He couldn't blame her, if she was.

Marlon shrugged. "I want to play, whether it's with the Monarchs or another team. But as long as I'm in Brooklyn, if the Monarchs are willing to extend my contract, I'm fine with staying here."

"That's not exactly a ringing endorsement of your commitment to the team." Her tone was dry.

"I'd be more excited if we were winning." He smothered the irritation that stirred inside him.

The look on Zerleena's face questioned his sanity. "Jackie Jones didn't trade for you so she could present you with a championship ring. She expects you to help the team win another title. What're you doing to help?"

"I'm coming off the bench. What more can I do other than cheer? And, look, while we're six-and-seventeen, there's not much to cheer about."

Zerleena gave him a half smile. "You're referring to the Monarchs as 'we.' That's a hopeful sign."

Pressure eased from Marlon's shoulders as the teasing lights returned to Zerleena's eyes. "So would you agree we have something to celebrate?"

Zerleena shifted her gaze to her glass of ice water. Her fingers traced an imaginary pattern through its condensation. "You're not going to ask me to marry you again, are you?"

He should have expected her question. He'd put her in an awkward position before. It was understandable she'd be even more cautious this second time around.

"No, Leena. I've learned my lesson." Marlon

searched his mind for the right words to express his heart. He couldn't blow it with her a third time. "I'm enjoying getting to know you, the person you've become." He cast his eyes around the restaurant. Several nearby diners quickly looked away. "I'm impressed by all you've accomplished. I want to continue to get to know you again. Would that be alright?"

Zerleena's smile warmed every atom of his body. "Of course."

Their server brought their entrees, interrupting their conversation. Marlon ate a forkful of the curried chicken. He hummed in pleasure as the seasoned meat slapped his taste buds awake. "This is fantastic."

"I know. The chef's a friend. I jumped at the chance to invest when she told me she wanted to open her own place."

"You're a part owner?" So his impression had been right. Marlon looked around the restaurant with fresh eyes. He knew he didn't have the right to be, but he was proud of her. "Your bio on your website's pretty sketchy—"

"You were on my website?" Zerleena paused with a forkful of rice and peas halfway to her mouth.

Why was she so surprised? "Yes, but like I said, your bio's pretty thin. How did you create Zerleena's She Shed?"

Her laughter was restrained as though she felt self-conscious. "I didn't plan on it. I went back for my master's. As you can imagine, student debt was crushing me. I came up with some budgeting and saving

tips that I shared with my girlfriends, including buying men's products."

"You told your girlfriends to buy men's products?"
Marlon raised a skeptical eyebrow. "Why?"

"Have you heard of the 'pink tax'?" Zerleena smiled
when Marlon shook his head in increasing confusion.
"It's not a literal tax. It refers to gender-based price
discrimination. Let's use antiperspirants as an example. A company will take one batch and market it
for men. They'll take another batch and market it for
women. It's basically the same product. The only difference is the one for women has a prettier fragrance
and is in a more attractive box. They use that to jus-
tify charging us more."

"You're kidding."

"I'm not. There are other examples of gender-based
economic discrimination. Look it up. My friends en-
couraged me to write a book with my advice on budgeting, investing, and navigating the banking and
finance industries. So I did, and when the book did
surprisingly well, I tried a workshop. When that was
successful, I launched my radio show."

"I can understand why your show's so popular. You
explain things so even people who don't have a clue
can understand and follow your advice."

That same surprised expression widened her eyes.
"You've listened to my show?"

"I'm interested in everything you do, Leena. I know
I have a lot of catching up to do."

Zerleena's gaze slipped away. Marlon had the impression she wanted to but didn't completely believe him. He was undaunted. Now that he knew he had the option to extend his contract with the Monarchs, he had time to make up for past mistakes and prove his sincerity.

"I like the theme of your upcoming workshop, 'Love Your Finances.'" Marlon looked up as the server appeared to refill their drink glasses.

"It seemed appropriate for the Valentine's Day scheduling. I just presented a workshop before Thanksgiving to help people prepare for the holiday shopping season. That one was The Gift of Budgeting. Love Your Finances deals with preparing for the tax season as well as the fallout from holiday spending."

Marlon spent the rest of the dinner encouraging Zerleena to share more about her workshops, show, and books. Each answer sparked several more questions from him, but she didn't seem to mind. She was interesting, informative, and always entertaining, just as she'd been in college. But this more mature Zerleena exuded a confidence that made her compelling. Even more, she was enthusiastic and passionate about her work. Her feelings were contagious. She could make him love financial planning. Almost.

Their conversation continued as he drove her home. Marlon glanced at her beside him. She seemed so relaxed and ... happy. "Your schedule is full, but you can't work all the time. What do you do to unwind and have fun?"

Zerleena turned to him with a mischievous smile. "Have dinner with friends."

He laughed. "You must do more than that."

"Not really. I have a couple of girlfriends. We've known each other for years. We get together every Sunday and take turns hosting brunch." Zerleena chuckled. "Some of us take a little more care with the menu than others."

Marlon wondered at the memory that prompted her smile. He wanted to share it. Amusement twinkled in her eyes and made her heart-shaped face almost glow. Her building came into view. His shoulders tensed. He didn't want the evening to end.

"Would you like to come in for a drink?" She made the question seem almost casual.

His prayer had been heard and answered. "Yes, I would. Thanks."

Marlon guided his car to her condo building's underground visitors' parking garage, which her father had pointed out to him. He found a spot for his car, then road the elevator up to her condominium. In the confined space, the warmth of her smile, and her soft, floral scent had the contradictory effect of relaxing and exciting him. The air was charged. Could she feel it? A random comment, an occasional glance eased the silence between them.

When the elevator doors opened, Marlon stepped back so Zerleena could exit first. Her long cream woolen coat masked her figure. His eyes skimmed the heavy garment, seeing in his mind's eye her figure-hugging dress with the side-split that teased him. He fisted his hands as the memory of holding her hips burned his palms.

Zerleena stood her brown handbag on the antique tobacco console just inside her entryway, then took his coat. The black cashmere garment disappeared into the closet with hers.

"What would you like?" She turned to him. "Coffee? Tea? Something stronger?"

"You." Marlon's response was unplanned, but right. It was what he was feeling. Had been feeling for months. "All I want is you, Leena."

She sighed as she closed the distance between them. "I want you, too, Marl."

Marlon closed his eyes. *Thank God.*

The last time they'd come together, their long-denied desire had exploded, consuming them like a wildfire. He'd loved it. He'd loved the way she'd taken control, had driven their passion. But this time, he wanted to take it slowly. Tonight, he wanted to savor their need for each other.

Marlon settled his hands on her waist, letting his eyes move over her again. "You look amazing in this dress."

Zerleena smiled. "It's not the dress. It's your imagination."

"I have a very vivid one." He swept her off her feet and into his arms. Her gasp of surprise made him smile. "That doesn't mean you don't look amazing."

She returned his kiss as he carried her down the

hall and into her bedroom. Her thigh stroked the length of him as he released her legs. He groaned deep in his throat. His mouth went dry as he watched her catch her plump lower lip between her teeth. Taking their time, they undressed each other between slow kisses and lingering caresses. His throat went dry at the sight of her standing naked in front of him.

"You're so beautiful." He didn't recognize his voice.

Her dark eyes glowed. "I can look at you forever."

He folded her against him, tracing kisses along her neck and shoulders. She drew her fingertips up his spine, flattening her palms against his back.

Evening shadows lengthened in her bedroom. The silence was heavy, giving him the sense that they were the only two people in the world. The fragrance of her perfume combined with the scent of their desire. His head spun.

"Leena." He gasped her name into her ear and felt her tremble in his arms.

Marlon let himself fall backward onto her bed, bringing her with him. They landed with a bounce. Zerleena's startled laughter made him smile, easing some — but not all — of his painful arousal.

He rolled over with her, bracing himself above her on his forearms as they kissed. She was soft yet firm, sweet yet spicy, warm and wet. She drew her fingers down his back, leaving trails of heat over his skin and making his muscles shake. He deepened their kiss, desperate to express the want building inside him. The need that had never gone away.

Zerleena strained toward him. Her right hand worked its way between them. She held him, her grip soft and tight. Marlon's hips moved in her grasp. She stroked him, urging him on. He left her lips to kiss her jawline, her chin, her neck. He needed to clear his head. He wanted tonight to last. Zerleena released him and his breathing slowed.

She pressed her palms against his shoulders and whispered beside his ear. "Lay back."

Marlon followed her direction. She straddled him. He tensed. She lowered her head and her hair brushed torso like a sigh. He swallowed. Zerleena pressed hot kisses from his navel to his groin. He groaned. His head pressed back into his pillow.

Zerleena stroked her tongue along his length then drew him deeper into her mouth. Marlon's hips strained up from the mattress. His grip tightened on the quilt beneath him, the only thing anchoring him to the room. Zerleena toyed with him. Teased him. Made him feel things he'd never felt before. Made him want things he'd never wanted before.

He reared up from the mattress. With a brief flex of his muscles, he drew Zerleena up to him and rolled her into his arms.

Zerleena started. Marlon's languid foreplay hadn't prepared her for his sudden shift in direction. His tongue slipped past her parted lips. She sighed and sent her tongue in search of his. His hunger empowered her. Emboldened her. His large, hot hands stroked her curves, caressed her thighs, and molded her breasts. She groaned as his weight pressed her into the mattress.

Marlon moved down her body, pausing to taste her shoulders, suckle her breasts, lick her torso. He kissed her right hip, then her left. A pulse was beating between Zerleena's legs. She rocked her hips, eager for him to join with her. Marlon blew a gentle breath against the soft hairs at the juncture of her thighs. Zerleena's hips shot off her bed.

"Marl, come inside me. Now." Her command was hoarse.

"Not yet." Marlon caught her hips and kissed her there.

A flash of heat raced up Zerleena's body. Her head pressed into her pillow. Her eyes squeezed shut. "Marl!"

Wave after wave of pleasure broke over and inside her. Marlon held her as he found a rhythm to drive her passion. Zerleena's muscles drew tighter and tighter. Her hands fisted, pulling at her quilt. Her hips pumped faster and faster.

"Marl, I can't ..."

He deepened his kiss.

Zerleena's body stiffened and she shattered.

Marlon slipped between her thighs. He gripped her hips and joined with her, entering with one smooth, deep thrust. He found her rhythm and road the aftershocks of her climax. Zerleena threw back her head and gasped as she felt another wave of pleasure building.

She opened her eyes. They locked with his. Marlon's features were taut with hunger, sharp with desire. His eyes were dark with need. He wrapped his arms around her, lowering his head to kiss her nipples.

Zerleena threw her arms above her head, arched her breast into his mouth, and let go. With a final thrust, Marlon caught her.

***

How in the hell am I supposed to win this game?

Marlon stood on the court, his arms and legs spread wide as he defended Knicks guard Kemba Walker. Less than thirty seconds remained in game thirty-two of the eighty-two-game season. The Monarchs were 9-22, soon to be 9-23. The score was 101 to 89, Knicks.

How could the starters have let this happen?

It was the day after Christmas, for pity's sake. I could've really used one more gift.

Warrick, Vincent, and Serge were on the bench with the rest of the team. Marlon was on the court with Barron, Jamal, Anthony, and Roger Harris. He wanted to grab each Monarch starter and shake them like rugs. But he couldn't. He had to get in the zone. He'd wanted a win. At this point, he'd settle for the Knicks not scoring again.

With his peripheral vision, Marlon checked the other players. Barron guarded Dwayne Bacon at the left side perimeter while Anthony had Taj Gibson at the right. Roger blocked Mitchell Robinson at the post, and Jamal secured Jericho Sims and the ball in the paint.

Sims spun to pass the ball. Jamal caught him with a hard jab to his torso. The refs called the foul. The kid's fifth. Marlon gritted his teeth.

The shot clock shut off. The game clock paused at twenty-seven seconds.

Marlon lined up along the lane as Sims prepared to make his free throws. So much for preventing the Knicks from extending their lead. The stench of defeat hovered over the other Monarchs. That stink had never been on his teams. It had always come from his opponents. Marlon's gut dipped with revulsion. How could he win the season if the Monarchs had returned to their loser mindset? They kept sabotaging themselves.

Sims made one of his two free throws, bringing the score to 102 to 89.

The game clock resumed. Roger grabbed the rebound and sped to the midcourt line. The Knicks' Robinson was on his heels.

"Shake it off! You've got this!" Warrick was the eternal optimist.

Marlon wanted to point to the scoreboard. *We've got* nothing. Instead he took the other man's advice and shook it off. He sensed Walker trailing him.

Bacon blocked Barron at the short corner. Gibson and Sims boxed Anthony in at the low post. Steps away, Jamal stood, open and dazed.

Marlon snapped. "Jamal! Take position!"

The rookie snapped out of his trance as Roger took the shot from the three-point line. He missed. Jamal was flat-footed in the paint. Anthony scrambled for the rebound. The Knicks' Sims claimed it.

Marlon took off in pursuit.

Twenty seconds on the clock.

Sims kicked the ball to Walker. Walker shifted, forcing Marlon back as he dribbled. Marlon read his opponent's body language. Walker wasn't passing this ball. He planned to shoot. Marlon held his position, softened his knees and got ready to jump.

Fifteen seconds.

In the blink of an eye, Walker spun. Leaped. Marlon leaped with him. His feet bounded from the court. His body stretched. His muscles strained. He caught the ball. Barely. Claiming it with his fingertips, he stopped its trajectory. He landed on the hardwood court, the ball secured between his palms.

Knicks's fans groaned. The sound sped around Madison Square Garden, propelling Marlon forward. He wove his way past and around Knicks players, making a path to the midcourt.

Eleven seconds.

Just one more score. One more to close the gap.

"Clear the driving lane! Communicate!" DeMarcus shouted from the sideline.

Warrick clapped them on from his position beside their head coach. "Stay focused! Talk to each other!"

The Knicks gave chase as though every point was

life and death. Marlon raced up the court as though they were right. Roger shouted for their zone offense. Marlon formed a mental image of the play. He tossed a blind pass to Roger. The other man secured it on the move. The Monarchs point guard dribbled as Jamal hustled to the post. Marlon, Barron, and Anthony took their positions in and around the paint. Roger sent the ball to the post.

Eight seconds.

Jamal hesitated. In that second, the Monarchs lost momentum.

The ball bounced from the young guard's chest — into Sims's hands.

The Knicks' Sims dribbled twice before sprinting back down court, fueled by the exultant cheers and shouts of the home team's fans.

Marlon's skin burned with temper. *Are you kidding me right now?*

Six seconds.

They can't lengthen the lead. We can't let them.

Gritting his teeth, Marlon dug deep as he set off after Sims. Barron, Anthony, and Roger gave chase with Jamal in the rear. Marlon reached Sims first. Digging even deeper, he launched himself just as Sims leaped to extend the Knicks' lead.

No!

Straining higher, Marlon slapped the ball from Sims. Barron jumped to make the save. He threw the ball back to Marlon. Marlon grabbed it one-handed as he landed on his feet. Ignoring the Knicks, their fans, and even his teammates, Marlon sprinted up court. Faster than he'd ever needed to move before. In his periphery, he saw Warrick pump his fist on the sideline, cheering him on.

Marlon's heart raced. His breaths panted. He blocked the shouts. Ignored the screams. Fatigue? What fatigue? Sweat stung his eyes.

Players gained on him from behind. He felt their energy at his back. He blocked that, too.

Two seconds.

Marlon entered the paint. Steps from the post, he launched himself at the basket. Both hands on the ball, he stuffed it through the net. Two points.

The game slowed as Marlon dropped back to his feet. Barron grabbed the ball as it fell through the net. Marlon stepped away from the post.

The clock stopped. The buzzer sounded. Final score: Knicks 102, Monarchs 91.

Despite his best efforts, the team had lost. Bitterly, spectacularly lost. Marlon turned away in disgust. Anger rolled over him as he walked past Monarchs players, congratulating their Knicks opponents. He avoided eye contact with everyone as he stalked toward Vom 2 and the visitors' locker room.

He had to wash the sour taste of defeat from his mouth.

I have to get off this team.

Chapter 13

The tension in the Knicks' visitors' locker room beat against Marlon like a drum, notching up his already smoldering temper. The foul stench of losing lingered beneath the scents of soap, deodorant, and cologne.

"I don't understand you guys." The words burst free of him without intent. Marlon shrugged into his smoke gray shirt before facing the room. The Monarchs players were in varying states of dress. They seemed distracted. They were either in a trance or depressed. He didn't care which. "You know what it takes to win. You've done it before so you know how it feels. Why are you so set to screw it all up this season? Do you like being losers?"

"*Losers?*" Jamal bounced from the bench in front of his locker. "Who're *you* calling losers? The Waves were so fired up to dump you that they traded you to their division rivals and you're calling *us* losers?"

Marlon ignored him. "You're getting used to losing again. It's like losing is your self-fulfilling prophecy. It's comfortable and familiar to you. There's just one problem: I'm on this team now too, and I don't want it to become comfortable or familiar for me."

"And it's always all about you, isn't it, Burress?" Anthony sneered his rhetorical question. At least Marlon thought it was rhetorical.

Jamal jerked his chin toward Marlon. "You think you're some kind of hero just because you made that final basket? You're not anyone's hero. Got that?"

Typical Jamal. It hadn't taken long for Marlon to realize when confronted, the kid jumped in with an attack to deflect from his poor play. Marlon wasn't having it tonight.

He hooked his hands on his hips and pinned Jamal with a scathing glare. "Why have you been sleepwalking through the games?"

"What d'you mean, I've been sleepwalking?" Jamal raised his voice. "There's nothing wrong with Jam-On-It's game, benchwarmer."

Marlon continued buttoning his shirt. "You froze during the game. More than once. You were like a deer in headlights. You either mentally check out, don't know the plays, or both. Which is it?"

Jamal's face flushed a deep, angry red. He jabbed a shaking finger toward Marlon. "I didn't check out of the game, *benchwarmer*. Jam-On-It never checks out of a game. Know that."

It took some effort, but Marlon refrained from rolling his eyes. "You've either fouled out or come close to fouling out of every one of the games. What's that about?"

Jamal threw his antiperspirant back into the locker. The resulting noise was a loud, disjointed clatter. Marlon didn't react. Instead he buttoned his shirt as he waited for Jamal to speak.

"I can't help it if the refs don't like me." He sounded like a petulant child.

Marlon couldn't handle it. He looked away. He turned his gaze to each Monarch in turn. He was amazed no one had a response to Jamal's statement. "Am I missing something or is that the biggest load of bull anyone's ever shoveled?" He directed his question to the room.

Warrick closed his now-empty locker. "It's pretty ridiculous."

Vincent nodded. "Yeah, it is."

Serge shrugged. "He's used worse."

"True." Barron sat on his bench to put on his shoes.

Roger, Darius Williams, and the other players grumbled their agreements.

Now they were getting somewhere. "So what're you going to do about it, Jamal?"

"I'll tell you what I'm going to do." DeMarcus's voice silenced the room. His three-button, black Italian-cut suit looked almost as drained as he did. Tension radiated like a dark force around him.

Judging by the other men's reactions, Marlon wasn't the only one who hadn't noticed DeMarcus's sudden and silent arrival. No one else seemed to be breathing, either. These post-loss locker room sessions were getting way too common.

DeMarcus pinned Jamal with a warning glare. "If

you don't get your head in the game and keep it there, you'll be coming off the bench."

The news caused Marlon's pulse to leap. Jamal was going to be benched. There wasn't any doubt about that. Is it possible he'd then get the kid's starting spot?

He slid a look toward Barron. After he'd returned to the Monarchs, the team's captain had joined Marlon on the bench. That made Barron his competition for Jamal's starting position. But the other man didn't react as though he'd heard DeMarcus's warning to the young starter. Didn't he want his spot back?

Marlon returned his attention to their coach. In all their years of friendship, he'd never seen DeMarcus as angry as he'd appeared after every Monarchs loss.

"Jamal isn't the only one screwing up the season." DeMarcus's hard coal black eyes circled the cramped locker room, lingering on Anthony, Serge, and Marlon.

"That's right." Jamal pumped his fist as though the fact the entire team was messing up was cause to celebrate.

Marlon ignored the kid. DeMarcus's eye contact had shaken him. Was his friend signaling *he* was somehow damaging the team?

DeMarcus continued as though Jamal hadn't spoken and he hadn't just rocked Marlon's confidence. "I don't know whether we're losing because you got cocky after winning the preseason games or if you're returning to old habits because they're more comfortable."

When no one offered a response, DeMarcus dragged his hand over his tight curls. "I didn't think I'd be giving these lectures again. I thought after we earned the title last season, you'd keep the momentum going. Instead, we're right back where we started last season." He looked at each of them. "Is this what you want? Are you satisfied with a losing record? Because I'm not. If we have to change our starting roster to win, I'm fine with that. Are you?"

DeMarcus didn't wait for a reply. He didn't need one. He was the head coach. Marlon watched his old friend's stiff-legged gait as he marched from the locker room.

Why had DeMarcus looked at *him* when he'd said Jamal wasn't the only one hurting their season? He wasn't doing anything wrong. The games were already lost before he came off the bench. Did DeMarcus see the situation differently?

"Well, I guess we have our homework assignments." Anthony grabbed his gym bag before leaving the room.

"I ain't doing no damn homework." Jamal grumbled his resentment as he followed Anthony out the door.

Adjusting his gym bag on his right shoulder, Marlon crossed to the door. He hesitated before walking through.

What was this team doing to his legacy? Did he have enough time to fix it?

***

"Cornell will keep calling until you answer." Zerleena's mother's voice carried over her cell phone Thursday late afternoon. Jillian's tone bordered on exasperated.

Zerleena's chunky black landline sat on her living room's blonde wood corner table beside her. She stared at it as though it had floated up from a sewer. "I'm trying to decide which would be worse: answering his call or having him spend the next two hours with a ringing telephone as his entire program."

Her landline was her primary phone contact for general agencies, professional associations, and pestilence such as Cornell Redd; groups she didn't want having access to her cell phone.

"Well, folks, that was our fourth attempt to connect with Zerleena Chase." Cornell's running commentary came through her laptop. *"She still isn't answering. Will she or won't she? Stay tuned to find out."*

How many listeners had chosen not to? Or was his audience so easily entertained that the sound of a ringing phone was enough?

That would explain so much.

Cornell's monologue added to Zerleena's irritation as she navigated his taunts, her mother's commands, and the phone's summons at the same time.

Zerleena didn't consider Cornell her rival but he did. She paid attention to his satellite radio show to stay apprised of what he was doing and saying. On the other hand, the only thing her overprotective parent seemed to be getting from Cornell's show was high blood pressure. She sighed. Why couldn't her mother understand that by tuning into Cornell's program, she was doing more to help him than protect her? Another sigh.

Cornell had had a lot of bad shows, including giving inaccurate or incomplete information, or no information at all. But today's program was hands down his worst to date.

He'd presented to his audience his intent to get Zerleena's reaction to "bombshell news" he'd learned about her past. But he wouldn't reveal it until and unless she answered his call. This meant his audience had spent the first half hour of his four o'clock show listening to a ringing telephone because Cornell wanted an "authentic reaction."

Translation: He hoped to embarrass her.

"If you don't answer, you'll look like a coward." Jillian's voice had crossed into the Massively Irritated Zone. "A coward with something to hide."

Zerleena frowned at her mother through her cell phone. "What you're calling 'cowardice,' I'm calling caution. I don't know anything about this news he claims to have."

"Then answer the phone and find out." Jillian had been a vocal member of Camp Smack Down Cornell since the satellite radio show host had revealed his entire strategy to grow his audience consisted of attacking Zerleena.

At least her mother was consistent. Her position

was in keeping with her naturally confrontational personality. Zerleena preferred a strategic approach. Not all situations should be handled with a hammer when a glove would suffice.

"Well, folks, what do you think?" Cornell's voice was full of forced humor. "Is Zerleena Chase cowering behind her couch to avoid our call?"

Zerleena closed her eyes and shook her head. That kind of comment was certain to spike her mother's blood pressure in *three ... two ...*

"Leena." Jillian sounded as though she'd pushed Zerleena's nickname past clenched teeth. "For my sake. Answer. The. Phone."

Did her mother realize her daughter was a grown woman in her late thirties? "All right, Mom." She sighed as she disconnected their call.

The phone had stopped ringing, too, as Cornell opted out of leaving a message and prepared for his next redial. She took advantage of the comparative quiet to deliver a stern lecture to herself: *No matter what Corny says, I will* not *react.*

As if on cue, her phone rang again.

"Well, folks, this is our seventh attempt to reach Ms. Zerleena Chase. Let's see if the seventh time's the charm." Cornell sounded as though he was reaching the end of his patience.

Good.

Zerleena took a calming breath before picking up her landline. "Hello."

"Zerleena?" He sounded surprised — and amused.

"Zerleena Chase? Wow. Well, I was beginning to think you were never going to pick up. Guess I was wrong, right? Where've you been? Cowering behind your couch? Locked in your bathroom? Or in bed — alone — with the cover pulled over your head?"

Do not *react.* "Why are you calling?"

Cornell's chuckle sounded faked and forced. "I get it. You don't want to give away your hidey-hole in case you need to use it again, say after our little chat."

Zerleena remained silent. She wasn't going to repeat herself so she didn't have anything to say. Her mother, on the other hand, would probably have come up with some stinging rejoinder that would have made Cornell cry. Perhaps something like, *Once I get through with you, you'll be slinking back into the mud from which you came.*

Wait! Why didn't I think of that sooner?

Oh, to have her mother's sharp tongue for just one day — or even one hour.

Cornell's pause was a nonverbal squirm. "Well, have you been listening to my show today?"

"Yes." As much as it pained her to admit it, she wasn't going to lie.

"Oh." Cornell's voice was pleased. "Are you a regular listener?"

"I tune in when I need background noise." *That one's for you, Mom.*

Speculating on her mother's appreciation of the comment didn't lighten her mood, though. She wanted to get this over with so she could get back to work on her manuscript. As her knowledge of finances had grown, so had her catalog of books — and her sales.

Another pause. "Well, Zerleena, since you're a regular listener of my program, you heard my announcement this morning that I've learned something very interesting about you. Isn't that right?" He prompted when Zerleena didn't react.

Zerleena closed her eyes, breathing deeply to keep her impatience in check. She didn't have time for Corny's games. "Why are you calling?"

"Out of curiosity, why did it take you so long to answer?"

Zerleena stared at the device in question as though Cornell had lost his mind. "I didn't care that you were making your audience listen to a ringing phone. I still don't. Either get to the point or I'm hanging up."

"Well, okay, okay. I can hear you're excited to find out what news I'm talking about."

Zerleena's hand shook with the effort to restrain her impulse to slam down her phone and smash it against its receiver over and over and over again.

Cornell continued. "My stellar investigative research has uncovered some interesting information about your past. Care to guess what it is?"

Don't *react*. *Do. Not.* "Actually, I'm curious about something else, Cornell, and perhaps you can clear this up for *me*. Your show is supposed to give your audience financial management advice. How does researching my personal life help your listeners better manage their money?"

"Well, I'm trying to help *your* listeners with information about the person they're getting advice from."

Why had I answered his call and how am I going to get out of this?

"My bio's on my website, in my books, and printed in every one of my workshop program guides. I'm not keeping secrets from my audience."

"Are you sure about that?" Cornell's voice was mean.

Zerleena stilled. What was this information he claimed to have on her? She was beginning to grow concerned but she refused to let it show. Her fist tightened on the cordless receiver. "Very sure."

"Then your audience knows you were in an *intimate* relationship with Marlon Burress during your entire four years in college until he broke your heart by *dumping* you immediately after he'd graduated — right after he'd been drafted to the NBA?" Triumph magnified Cornell's voice.

Zerleena went cold. Her pulse pounded in her ears. She couldn't breathe.

How had he found out about her relationship with Marlon? Who had told him something so very personal about her?

Carol Mart.

Her former college roommate was the only person who'd known about her previous relationship with Marlon and would share that private information with her nemesis. And now Cornell had announced it to an audience of tens of thousands.

She saw red. Her blood started a slow simmer. Her muscles shook as her body heated.

Zerleena unclenched her teeth and loosened her fists. She needed to stay in control. She wouldn't confirm or deny Cornell's information. He wouldn't get any additional insights into her life. Just the thought of that troll having any personal information about her made her shiver with revulsion.

"Cornell, assuming your information is accurate, why should it be of any interest to my audience?"

"Having a successful, professional athlete break up with you after you gave him four years of your life would go a long way toward explaining why you hate men." Cornell lingered over every syllable of his explanation as though each was a sweet treat.

Zerleena drew a deep breath, filling her lungs and counting to ten. "As a rule, I don't hate anyone, Cornell. But I'd consider breaking that rule for you."

She cradled her landline with deliberate calm. It required a Herculean effort to do that while battling back the past insecurities, heartache, and resentment that tried to reclaim her.

Zerleena rose from the sofa to wander her living room. She ignored her cell phone's summons. It was probably her mother — or D.C. Either way, she wasn't ready to talk. Her mind had already tumbled down into the past.

When Marlon had dumped her, she'd spent a crap

ton of time trying to make sense of what had gone wrong. He'd been drafted to the NBA. Did that mean she wasn't good enough for him anymore? Wasn't she worth the effort of a long-distance relationship? After fifteen years, why did he think she was worth the effort now?

Or did he?

***

"The Mighty Guinn." Marlon's smile was mocking as he sauntered farther into DeMarcus's spacious silver-and-black office.

His coach tapped a series of keys on his computer before spinning his heavy black executive chair to face him. The former shooting guard was three years out of the league, but looked like he could still hold his own on the court. "I hate when you call me that."

"I know." Pleasantries over, Marlon dropped onto one of the three black cushioned seats in front of the massive oak desk. It was early January in Brooklyn, the start of a new year, but he couldn't decide whether it was colder outside or in DeMarcus's office. "I know money's tight in the franchise, man, but can't you afford some heat?"

DeMarcus's almond-shaped, coal black eyes baited him. "I guess your delicate Southeast blood hasn't adjusted to the Northeast climate."

"I was born and raised in Detroit. Remember?" Marlon scanned his surroundings. "But this is inhumane."

DeMarcus's office reflected the man. It exuded power and control like a winner. The framed photos on the paper white walls memorialized his three NBA titles and his two MVP honors. It also documented the Monarchs' improbable championship run last year. It was hard to square the reigning NBA champs with the dysfunctional team that had been showing up to this season's debacles. They were more like dribbling zombies, primed to eat their own if it raised their individual profiles.

Across the room, a small mountain of digital video discs was stacked on an oak conversation table surrounded by black cushioned chairs. A tall, leafy green plant stood beside an overburdened oak bookcase. It looked fake.

Marlon was happy, seeing his friend doing so well. Both DeMarcus and Steven were successful and, more importantly, happy in their life-after-basketball careers.

Walter Millbank, another retired teammate and mutual friend, also was happy with the health spa in Colorado that he and his wife had launched. At least, he was as happy as he could be married to Tracee Greer Millbank. Marlon winced on the inside. She was extra ... everything. But Walter loved her. Wasn't that what mattered?

The three men gave him hope for his after-basketball life. He just wished he knew what that life looked like.

His attention returned to DeMarcus. Part of him

understood their relationship had to change. They weren't peers anymore. DeMarcus was his head coach. But another part of him wished it didn't have to be that way. DeMarcus had been his friend for more than a decade.

"We're halfway through the season, Marc. We're the reigning NBA champs and the team's eleven and twenty-eight after last night's loss. At home. To a team with more Ls than us." His throat burned with shame. The Waves had never fallen to a team with such a poor standing. For him, this was a new low.

"I know our record." DeMarcus leaned back against his chair and propped his right ankle on his left knee. He returned Marlon's searching gaze with an enigmatic look.

Same old Marc. Marlon flashed a quicksilver grin. "You've gone all sphinxy on me. I hate when you do that."

"I know." A smile relaxed the other man's sharp sienna features.

DeMarcus still had the best poker face in the NBA. It had been one of his most effective weapons, that and his will. Their opponents couldn't read him, which made it almost impossible to anticipate the Mighty Guinn's moves.

It was late Tuesday afternoon. The Monarchs had just finished their practice. It was more of a walk-through than a workout, in keeping with a practice session sandwiched between two games. Tomorrow, they were hosting the Milwaukee Bucks in the Empire Arena. Would they extend their losing streak to six?

He couldn't believe that was even a possibility. "In my entire career, I've never lost six straight games. I've never lost even half that in a row."

DeMarcus's smile faded. "I know."

"How much longer are you going to let this go on, Marc?" He searched DeMarcus's dark eyes and lean features. "It's time to make a change, man." If the team didn't make a change — and soon — Marlon was afraid he'd never get the bitter taste of defeat out of his mouth.

DeMarcus's gaze remained impassive. "Go ahead."

The invitation lacked enthusiasm, but Marlon accepted anyway. "What more's there to say? What you're doing isn't working. We aren't even pretending to be a team. We're thirteen guys wearing the same clothes, standing on the same court."

"I know." DeMarcus sighed. In anger or disgust? Did it matter?

"You know. You know. You know." Did DeMarcus think those words were reassuring? They weren't. Instead they were fueling his frustration. "What're you going to do about it?"

DeMarcus was silent.

The rhythmic tapping that was so irritating was coming from him. Marlon stopped drumming his fingers against his chair's metal arm. "I want more playing time."

DeMarcus inclined his head. "You're a competitor. All competitors want more playing time."

Emboldened, Marlon continued. "You're not using me enough. I can do more to help the team. But I'd have to come in before the second quarter. By then, it's too late. Too much damage has been done."

DeMarcus was silent for another long moment. Was he taking time to think about his response — or giving Marlon time to reconsider his request?

When he finally spoke, his words were measured as though he was entering new ground. "The team's got a lot of talent."

"Yes, it does." Marlon could give credit where credit was due.

"Jamal's fast. Serge's strong on defense. Rick's accurate from anywhere and everywhere on the court."

Marlon picked up the list. "Vinny has vision and Tony has power, but they're still losing."

"We aren't losing because we lack talent." DeMarcus cocked his head. "Do you know why we're losing?" He was impersonating Laurence Fishborne's character, Morpheus, from the futuristic sci-fi movie *The Matrix*. And he was doing it poorly.

Marlon smothered a sigh. "No, Morpheus. Why is the team losing?"

"Because we aren't playing like a team." DeMarcus spread his hands. "You've said it yourself. Thirteen guys in the same clothes, standing on the same court."

Marlon popped out of his seat and threw his arms wide. "You're making my argument for me."

"No, you're making mine." DeMarcus lifted his chin to maintain eye contact. "These guys have been teammates for years, but they still don't trust each other enough to play together. So how would you — a new teammate who was traded from our division rival — do any better on the court with them when they don't trust you at all?"

Marlon hated to admit it, but DeMarcus had a point. He circled his chair to pace the office. "Those guys would become used to having me in the game if I had more playing time."

DeMarcus laughed. "They haven't accepted you in *practice.* Granted you're a lot to get used to, but before I extend your playing time, you're going to have to get the team to accept you."

"How do I do that?"

"Win the locker room, Marl."

Marlon scowled. He'd never had to worry about that before. He'd been with the Waves his entire career. He'd fit into the locker room by virtue of his being an effective part of their winning strategy.

How do I win the locker room when the team's losing?

"So I'm just supposed to watch these debacles from the bench?"

"For now."

Marlon's scowl deepened. "You know I can be effective in turning this shit show around."

DeMarcus shook his head. "Baby steps, Marl. It starts in the locker room."

Marlon started to leave. At the door, he turned back to DeMarcus. "You knew what I'd wanted to talk with you about, didn't you?"

"Yes."

"Then why'd you let me say all that if it wasn't going to change your mind?"

"Jack thought you'd need to get it off your chest. She believes emotional support is as important as physical preparation for a team's success." From the lack of inflection in DeMarcus's voice, Marlon sensed he wasn't completely on board with his fiancée and franchise owner in this instance. "Just win the locker room, Marl."

Win the locker room. Marlon turned to leave.

How?

Chapter 14

"On-It, you're killing us!" Marlon fought with himself to stay off the court at the Miami Waves Arena Friday night. It wasn't easy.

"Shut up, grandpa!" The ball hog glared at him after taking another wild shot — and missing it.

He couldn't watch the second-year ego miss another basket. The kid must have the worst field goal percentage in the league. The next time he spoke with Jaclyn Jones, he was going to ask why she'd drafted him.

Marlon ignored him as he rallied his team. "Let's get it back. Stay focused. We can do this!"

Could they really?

No one would call this a game. It was a thrashing of epic proportions. The Monarchs were on the precipice of extending their inglorious six-game losing streak to seven. Courtesy of their division rival Waves, after tonight, their record would drop to 11-30, including their home game loss to the Milwaukee Bucks Wednesday.

Marlon felt sick. "Talk to each other! You don't even have to pick up the phone. You're right there together on the court!"

Marlon wanted to beat his former team so badly he

could taste, smell, hear, and feel it. But reality stared him down. The Waves led 91-77 with four minutes left to the game. Winning was impossible, but giving up was worse.

"Stay on him, Tony!" He watched his bible-quoting forward deny his assignment a clear shot to the basket. "His left side's weak."

He didn't care whether one of the many cameras recording the debacle would capture his courtside meltdown. It was either roar like a wounded animal or sob like a child. Even DeMarcus had lost his legendary poker face.

"Jamal!" DeMarcus sounded like he was chewing glass. "Get your head in the game."

The shooting guard was the biggest problem the Monarchs had. He was either sleepwalking all over the court like a zombie or hogging the ball like he was Gladys Knight and the other Monarchs were the Pips — in the same game. Both routines made Marlon want to charge the court and snatch the ball from him.

He'd run some plays and scored a few points just before the half and at the beginning of the third quarter. That was before the Monarchs had gone off the rails, allowing the Waves to score at will.

Marlon clenched his teeth. Jamal had gone back to sleepwalking through his minutes. He'd missed Vincent's pass. Again. For pity's sake. As many times as the kid botched that play, why did the Monarchs keep running it? He wanted to shake the young guard until his teeth rattled. As that fantasy sparked in his mind,

Warrick materialized out of thin air. Marlon clenched his fists, adding his will to the veteran shooting guard's.

He watched the six-six baller strain forward, snatching the ball from the narrow space between Jamal and his Waves shadow. Marlon tightened his fist and gritted his teeth as two opponents turned their attention to his teammate. Warrick spun on his toes, evading those defenders and allowing Marlon to breathe. Vincent and Serge raced to cover the veteran's back. Warrick soared toward the basket. Two points. Monarchs 79, Hawks 91.

Marlon's relief was intense. He leaped from the ground, pumping his arm. "Yes! Yes! Rick, man, *that's* what we mean." He applauded, though Warrick remained focused on the game and had transitioned to defense. He shifted his attention to the younger guard. "Yo, On-It, *that's* how you play basketball."

Jamal cut a venomous look to Marlon. Was that expression meant to shut him up? Marlon threw back his head and laughed.

Sensing an audience, he turned to find DeMarcus regarding him with irony. "What?"

DeMarcus shook his head with a smile. "It's good to see you cheering on the team, even if your main motivation is pissing off your teammates."

"Not all of them. Just Jamal." Marlon turned back to the court. "Pick up the pace, On-It!"

"Shut up, old man." Jamal sounded like he was crunching glass with his teeth.

Marlon winked at DeMarcus. "But stop calling that skip play. Jamal's not working it."

He turned back to the court in time to see the Waves miss their last basket at the buzzer. The torture had ended 91-79, Waves. Marlon looked across the court at his former teammates, elated in victory. He nodded to his head coach as a few of the players before following his new team into Vom 2. *Next time.*

Minutes later, Marlon stood in the visitors locker room taking small breaths to keep from passing out from the abundance of Jamal's cologne. Marlon breathed gingerly.

"I was surprised you'd cheered for us that hard against your former team." Vincent broke the brooding silence.

Jamal snorted. "What else is the old man supposed to do from the bench?"

Marlon ignored the second-year ego and glanced over his shoulder at Vincent. During the last forty games, wins and losses, the six-eight shooting guard had never initiated a post-game conversation. He was the quietest player on their roster. He rarely spoke, except to antagonize St. Anthony.

He turned back to his locker. "I wanted the W."

"I appreciate it, man." Vincent stood to leave.

Marlon grabbed his gym bag to follow him. If DeMarcus was going to storm into the locker to deliver another lecture on their dysfunctional team chemistry, he would've done it by now.

Warrick stopped him with a hand on his shoulder. "Thanks, man. It helped, despite the final score."

Marlon's eyebrows knitted. He looked around the locker room and saw the other players regarding him with something that approached comradery. At least, it was a much friendlier expression than their previous open hostility.

He turned back to the team captain. "Next time."

Marlon turned. He sensed Warrick behind him as he walked out the door. *So this is how you win the locker room?* It had been much easier than he'd thought.

***

Erika's expression was a portrait of disappointment. "Are you ever going to put any effort into these brunches?" She shifted her attention from the watery porridge sitting in a pink porcelain bowl to Keysha and back.

It was the final Sunday in February. The trio was gathered around Keysha's Plexiglas-and-metal kitchen table. When Zerleena and Erika had arrived, Keysha's kitchen had smelled of strong coffee and lemon dishwashing liquid. A very bad sign. In fact, this brunch may have been their friend's worst hosting effort ever.

"There's fruit." Keysha's voice squeaked with defensiveness. She looked fit and comfortable in a thick crimson sweater and navy yoga pants. She'd accessorized with a long gold necklace and matching dangling earrings. If only she'd paid as much attention to their meal.

"From a can." Zerleena tried but failed to keep the amusement from her voice.

"And fresh juice." Keysha's eyes wavered under Erika's shaming expression. "Well, freshly made this morning from frozen concentrate. But, Erika, not everyone can whip up magic like you — although Zerleena comes close."

"My talents are nowhere near as legendary as Erika's skills, which is one of the reasons we invested in Manny's Caribbean Cuisine." Zerleena took a deep drink of coffee. Keysha's coffee was her redeeming feature.

"Speaking of changing the subject." Keysha gave Erika a pointed look before waving a spoonful of porridge toward Zerleena. "How're you going to respond to Corny's latest attack against you? That poser needs to be punished."

"No doubt." Erika stopped playing with her porridge. She nudged aside the bowl and reached for the cup of mixed fruit. "I know some people."

Zerleena considered Erika sitting quietly in a demure dark floral sweater dress. "You keep saying that. Do you really have connections to enforcers?"

Erika slid a look toward Keysha, their resident attorney, and smiled.

Zerleena sat back on the black-vinyl-and-silver-metal chair. She looked from Erika to Keysha. "Don't tell me you're both still listening to Corny's show."

"Know your enemy, girl." Keysha shrugged her shoulders. "We need to do *something*. We can't continue to let his crap go unchallenged."

"He could get roughed up outside his house." Erika finished eating her fruit.

"Or leave a horse's head in his bed." Zerleena's tone was dry.

"That's old school." Erika drew Keysha's fruit bowl toward her. She stopped the other woman's objections with a look.

Zerleena gave Erika a concerned look. She sounded kind of serious. Shaking off the thought, she crossed to Keysha's fridge. "Marl offered to speak with him, but I asked him not to get involved."

Marlon was fresh off his fourteenth appearance in the NBA All-Star game. Since he'd been coming off the bench, the invitation had surprised him. Warrick had been selected as well. This was the Monarchs star's first appearance and long overdue. She shrugged off a sense of righteous indignation.

In other fantastic news, the team had turned their season around. They were playing the Sixers in Philly tonight. If they won this game and the next, which was at home against the Chicago Bulls, their record would be tied at 30 wins and 30 losses with twenty-two games left in the regular season. Zerleena could smell the faint but real possibility of a play-off berth.

Please. Please. Please.

"You're right." Keysha sounded distracted. "Marl's intervention would do more harm than good."

"Now, if Marl wanted to rough him up, I'd be all in with that." Erika stared into the empty fruit bowl, her expression forlorn. Perhaps hunger had put the extra edge in her imagery.

Zerleena turned back to Keysha's fridge with an even greater sense of urgency. "No one's going to rough anyone up."

"Killjoy." Erika's grumpy response didn't provide any clues as to whether she was serious.

"What're you looking for?" Keysha asked.

Zerleena rescued a decimated loaf of bread. "I'm making toast. Want some?"

"I do!" Erika closed her eyes in relief.

Zerleena put the last three slices of bread in the toaster. "D.C. thinks I should call Corny myself and have an on-air showdown."

A spark of interest brightened Keysha's dark eyes. "Do it."

Erika gave an evil grin. "Yes."

"I don't want to have a shouting match with Corny on live radio." Zerleena buttered the toast, split one-and-a half slices between two plates, then returned to the table. "That would damage my brand."

"Brand, spland." Erika scoffed as she accepted the toast with a hint of impatience. "Thank you."

Keysha gaped at them. "Where's mine?"

Erika shoved her untouched bowl of porridge across the table and spoke around a mouthful of warm, buttery toast. "You can eat the watery porridge." She pushed Zerleena's porridge closer to their hostess as well with a look that dared her to object.

Keysha squared her shoulders and faced a second bowl of porridge with resignation. "You're worried about doing something that will hurt your brand, but Corny's already doing a job on it."

Erika nodded. "You *talk* about empowering women on your program, in your books, and your workshops. But you don't *show* it. You let this Corny guy spew his nonsense and don't stand up for yourself."

The words stung like a slap across her face. The fact her friend was right made it hurt worse.

"I'm the one who's hurting my brand." She dropped her half-eaten slice of toast back onto the plate. "I have to fix this."

"Truth." Keysha pilfered the toast from her plate. "Ignoring him isn't making him go away."

Erika jerked the toast from Keysha's hand before the other woman could take a bite. She nodded toward the porridge. "Whaddya gonna do with that?"

Keysha frown. "Guess I'll throw it out."

"Let that be a lesson to you." Erika handed the toast back to Zerleena. "Because you're being so meek, his attacks are escalating."

Zerleena squeezed her eyes shut. Erika was right. Again. *Urgh.* "Alright. No more diplomacy. The gloves are coming off."

"Now you're talking." Erika rubbed her hands together. "What's the plan?"

She pursed her lips. "I need to call in a few favors."

***

"The Waves have made an offer for my contract." Marlon stood in the center of Zerleena's living room Tuesday afternoon to deliver his news. It was March and he spoke with exuberance as though he was presenting her with the Monarchs first back-to-back championship titles in franchise history.

She frowned. "They want you back?"

"I couldn't believe it, either." Marlon's dark eyes shone. Waves of joy swept off him and battered her but couldn't penetrate the wall of tension surrounding her.

Bells clanged in her ears and her head spun when she realized Marlon thought his returning to his old team was the greatest news he could give her. How surprised would he be to learn he wasn't even close? In fact, his returning to Miami wasn't on the list.

Good ol' Marl. Clueless as ever.

For the past three months, she'd foolishly thought they were moving toward a second chance together. How could she have been so stupid again? He hadn't been building anything with her. He'd been using her: a sympathetic ear to listen to him; an enthusiastic fan to cheer him; a warm body to hold in bed. And now, while his joy burst through his pores, her heart shattered in her chest.

She dropped her eyes to his black Monarchs jersey,

straining across his chest. He'd won the locker room. The team had started winning. At 38-32 with 12 games left, they were in position to make it to the playoffs. Yet all he could think about was returning to Miami and leaving her behind.

The bitter taste of disappointment collected in her throat. She had to force it back before she could speak. "When will you have the Monarchs' decision?"

"It should only take a few days. I'd complete the season with the Monarchs but next year, I could be with the Waves again."

How could he sound so happy? Couldn't he see he was killing her? Of course not. He couldn't see anything beyond himself. She'd been an idiot not to remember that.

You let your guard down, Leena. Now you're paying the price.

She wandered toward her plant menagerie, struggling to rebuild her defenses against him and the way he made her feel. The hardwood was cool beneath her bare feet. The warmth of the late afternoon sun washed over her through her picture window. "And you're certain you want to go back to the Waves? They traded you before. How do you know you can trust them this time?"

Just as you broke my heart years ago. I'd been stupid to trust you with it again.

Marlon hesitated. "The Waves have been my home for the past fifteen years. It's where I belong."

"Is it?" Zerleena could almost smell his uncertainty.

Her eyes stung. With her back to him, she squeezed them shut, fighting back tears. Her stomach churned with ... Anger? Hurt? Both?

"What's wrong, Leena?" She hadn't heard his approach, but his voice sounded closer. Softer. "I thought you'd be happy."

Zerleena squared her shoulders before turning to face him. He was close, too close. She took a step back, just beyond his reach. "Happy for whom?"

Marlon frowned. "For us."

Zerleena narrowed her eyes. Was he serious? He was serious. Wow!

How could he think the news of his impending move out of Brooklyn — away from her — could make her happy? "What *us*, Marl? How could there be an *us* when one of *us* is planning to leave?"

Marlon's expression cleared. His broad grin was like the sun coming out from behind rain clouds. Zerleena wished there were curtains she could shut to cover his face.

"Leena, did you think I was leaving without you?" He chuckled as though the thought amused him. "I'm not letting you go this time. You're coming with me."

Zerleena stepped back again, shaking her head. The man was so galactically dense. Maddeningly clueless. Stupendously unaware. "Wait. What? You thought you'd come into my home, announce you were moving to Miami, and I'd pack my bags? And you made this assumption without asking me?"

Marlon's confusion returned. "We're together

again. I'm not going to make the same mistake I made before, Leena. I want you in my life."

"Of course. *Your* life." She lifted a hand, palm out, and traced a circle with it in front of his face. "Because this is all about *you*, isn't it, Marl?" She dropped her arm. "It's *always* all about *you*."

She shoved Marlon aside to march past him. Her temper spiked when her push didn't moved him. Instead he stepped aside for her. Anger carried her across the room in long, stiff strides. Her skin was hot, her breathing labored. Her chest rose and fell as she strained for control.

"Leena, that's not fair. Come on, talk to me. Why're you upset?"

Zerleena barely heard Marlon's anxiety above the blood rushing in her head. She paced in front of her smoke gray loveseat. "I can't *believe* I have to explain this to you." She sent him a scathing look as she chewed the words. "You consider Miami to be your home. Your parents are there. You have friends there. Well, Brooklyn is *my* home, Marl. I have family and friends *here*. My career is *here*."

Marlon spread his arms. His dark eyes were clouded with confusion as though he still couldn't fathom her objections. "But, Leena, you can write books, host workshops, and do your satellite radio program from anywhere."

Zerleena's eyes almost crossed with shock and fury. "Didn't you just have to relocate when the Waves traded you to Brooklyn?"

"Yes, but—"

Zerleena cut him off. "I'm stunned you're so disconnected to the upheaval something like that plays on a person's life, especially when they don't have any say and very little notice. You just went through the same thing."

"I know it's a lot, but—"

"The conference center that hosts my workshops. The offices for my satellite radio program. My production intern. They're all *here*."

Marlon's eyes wavered as though he was starting to sense the enormity of his request. "Leena, I know it's asking a lot, but if you care about me, it wouldn't be too much for you to make the effort."

Was steam billowing from her ears? It was a distinct possibility. "That's the thing, Marl. If *you* cared about *me*, you would've asked first instead of taking for granted that I'd agree to move."

A cloud of temper swept across his chiseled features. "Is it really so much to expect you to want to make the effort?"

Zerleena had lost the battle with her temper. She'd allowed Marlon Burress to make a fool of her. Again. It had taken her years to even start to heal the wound he'd given her after their first breakup. This time, she knew it would take so much longer.

"If you'd shown *any* consideration of my feelings instead of taking my compliance for granted, then I'd think you were worth the effort. But since you demonstrably didn't think about how a move would affect *me*, then I'm thinking I don't need to uproot myself and move almost thirteen hundred miles away for the convenience of someone who sees me as a sperm receptacle. Any paper cup would do. Right, Marl?"

"Where the hell did that come from?" Marlon dragged both hands over his tight curls.

"What am I supposed to think?" She threw up her arms, struggling not to screech like a fire truck, speeding to put out a blaze. "I didn't even know you were still looking to be traded. After you told me Jaclyn Jones said you have a spot on the team, I thought you were going to stay in Brooklyn. Then you show up at my door, talking about *us* moving to Miami and what a great thing this would be for *us*. Where did *that* come from?"

"You're right." Marlon's voice was tight as though he also was making an effort to keep from airing their differences for her neighbors' entertainment. "After Jackie said she wanted me on the team, I stopped looking to be traded, but my agent didn't."

"You didn't tell him you wanted to stay here in Brooklyn?" *That you wanted to stay with me?*

Marlon shook his head. "I didn't think about it."

"You mean, you didn't think about *me*." Her voice was graveled with pain and anger.

"Oh, come on, Leena. That's not what I said or meant. This opportunity just presented itself."

"And you leaped on it. If you believed in *us*, you would've stopped to consider *me*."

"Leena—"

"Enough!" She spun on her bare heels and marched toward her front door. "I can't discuss this any longer. Please leave."

Marlon reached for her as she drew closer to him. "Leena, I want—"

Zerleena dodged his hand. "*You* want. I'm so sick of hearing that. I want, too. I want someone who thinks about me, perhaps once a week. Is that too much to ask?"

Without waiting for his answer, she yanked open the front door. She swept her left arm forward, gesturing for him to leave.

Marlon started to speak. Perhaps it was the look in her eyes that made him reconsider. Whatever it was, he realized she wasn't going to hear anything more he had to say. He crossed her threshold and stepped out of her life.

Zerleena closed the door after him. Pressing herself against the wall, she slid to the floor. Tears flooded her eyes and spilled down her cheeks. Sobs ripped from her gut and clawed out of her throat. She hadn't meant to give him the power to break her heart again. Could she find the strength to heal this time?

Chapter 15

"We have a change in the lineup." DeMarcus looked at each of the players sprawled on the practice court's bleachers late Tuesday morning before settling his eyes on Jamal. "Barron's starting. Jamal's coming off the bench."

That explained why Jamal had been slamming around the team's practice locker room and sending Barron dirty looks from across the court all morning. It also explained why Barron was in the black T-shirt given to starters while Jamal was bare chested. The two men must have met with DeMarcus prior to practice.

Oscar Clemente, the Monarchs's first assistant head coach, stood in his usual position beside DeMarcus. A man of few words, Oscar exuded approval and satisfaction. If Jamal protested DeMarcus's decision, he wouldn't find an ally with Oscar. And judging from the collective sigh that floated around the practice court, neither would he find support from his teammates.

Marlon's body dripped sweat from his ninety-plus minutes of warm up. He brought his attention to the bleachers. He looked from Jamal's mask of fury to Barron's enigmatic expression. He was happy for Barron.

He'd been playing his best game this season. At one time, he'd been the Monarchs captain before abdicating that position and supporting Warrick in a team vote.

Marlon had been playing his best game, too, though. His numbers were high. His skills were strong. He was one of the top-producing players on the team along with Warrick, Vincent, and Barron. And he'd finally won the locker rom. So why was he still riding the bench? And how much worse would that seat be with Jamal beside him?

Answer: A lot.

Jamal glowered around the practice court. "This is bull!"

His explosion was expected. What surprised Marlon was that it had taken as long as it had. "Why is it bull, On-It? Do you think you've been playing well?"

The younger player turned his venom on him. "Ain't nobody talkin' to you, old man. And stop calling me that."

Marlon didn't want to let the question go — or give up the altered nickname. "It's not like coach hadn't warned you more than once to step up your game or lose your spot. Did you think he was kidding?"

"I wasn't." DeMarcus's tone was dry as dust. He crossed his arms over his chest and stared at Jamal.

"I didn't think so." Anthony sounded like he was enjoying this moment.

"You couldn't have been surprised by Coach's decision." Warrick shifted to look at Jamal. He used a towel to dry the back of his neck. "You must've known you weren't playing well."

Serge snorted. "Everyone else did."

Marlon nodded. "I'm sure I'm not the only one who could track most of our losses to you."

Jamal's face flushed red. "How much game have you had, benchwarmer?"

"We're talking to you, On-It." Vincent wiped sweat from his forehead. His voice was low but he commanded everyone's attention. "You've been on autopilot, putting extra pressure on the rest of us. We deserve to know why you've been sleepwalking at work."

Jamal shot off the bleachers and leaped onto the court, spinning to face the team. Marlon's eyes stretched wide. The kid had demonstrated more speed and energy in the last minute than he'd shown in months. Even the ink covering the kid's wiry six-foot-four-inch frame seemed outraged.

He jabbed a finger in the general direction of the team. "*Jam*-On-It can outplay all of you washed-up, washed-out has-beens. None of you can touch me."

Marlon rubbed his forehead. He could feel the initial drumming of a headache. "Just answer the question, man." *For pity's sake.*

Jamal fisted his hands. He scowled at the coaches who stood two arms' lengths from him and glowered at his teammates on the bleachers. Waves of emotion vibrated from him, battering Marlon: anger, tension, and ... fear?

Abruptly, his posture slumped as though all the fight and energy drained from him. His hands went slack. His sneakers squeaked against the high-gloss hardwood floor as he turned his back to the coaches to stare across the court toward the black wire carts of basketballs and the counters that balanced a dozen or so reusable water bottles.

Jamal mumbled something. Marlon couldn't make it out.

DeMarcus frowned, leaning forward. "What?"

"It's my girl!" Jamal spun to face the coach. Temper and uncertainty battled for control of his thin, young features. "She's been keeping me out late."

"On game nights?" Anthony's shocked question expressed the surprise and confusion of everyone in the gym.

Barron appeared disbelieving. "Does she know you're chasing the ring?"

Vincent gave him a look of exaggerated concern. "Damn, is she holding you against your will?"

"No!" Jamal spat his response.

Vincent cocked his head. "Then why don't you get up and leave?"

"Vinny's right." DeMarcus crossed his arms over his chest. The Monarchs logo was centered on his black nylon T-shirt. "If you want to go out with your girl, that's fine. But you can't stay out all night and expect to stay on this team. We're working for back-to-back titles. We need your mind and body on the court and on the bench. Full commitment. Nothing less."

Jamal blasted him with a glare. "I *am* committed."

"To your girl." Serge's words were scathing. "Coach means full commitment to the team."

DeMarcus nodded toward Jamal. "Get the white jersey."

Marlon watched Jamal shuffle toward the counter and the stack of jerseys for second-string players. He'd dated women who'd wanted to stay out all night, spending his money and using his fame for access to exclusive clubs. With those women, there hadn't been a second date. He'd always known what he'd wanted for his career: To be the best.

Things were different with Zerleena. She was more concerned than he was that he had a good night's rest before a game. On those nights, they'd stay in. Now that Zerleena had thrown him out of her life, he wasn't getting much sleep. Ironic.

"Is anyone else having trouble with people keeping them from focusing on the game?" DeMarcus's dry question pulled Marlon from his thoughts.

Slowly, hesitantly, Serge raised his hand. "There is one person who is causing for me some trouble."

DeMarcus's eyebrows rose. "Who?"

Serge looked around at the other players and coaches watching him. His reluctance to name the source of his discomfort was palpable and amusing. "Andrea Benson."

Soft chuckles bounced around the court. Andrea was dating Troy Marshall, the franchise's vice president of marketing. A huge Monarchs fan, she attended all the home games, sitting with the other players' wives and girlfriends in the rows behind the team.

Vincent laughed, shaking his head. "I feel you, Serge. I liked Andrea more when she was a sports reporter. Now that she's a newspaper columnist, she's lost all restraint when it comes to expressing her fandom."

Barron's grin was bashful. "Some of her comments are kind of hurtful."

"Hurtful?" Marlon snorted. "They're emasculating."

A smile pulled at DeMarcus's lips. He must've heard them too. "I'll speak with Troy."

***

"You and Marl broke up?" Keysha's lips parted in shock. She lowered her glass of wine and leaned into the table.

Erika's catlike eyes were wide. "Which one of you did the breaking up?"

Zerleena and her friends were meeting at a local restaurant Friday evening for drinks and appetizers. The meetup had prompted Erika to give herself a three-day weekend from her business. It was a rare treat, but Zerleena suspected her friend would spend most of her time on paperwork and stop by the restaurant at least once per day "to check on things."

It also gave Zerleena an excuse to take a break from

her manuscript, which was due Monday, and Keysha a reason to leave work at her busy law practice on time.

Zerleena shifted her attention from the spinach-and-artichoke dip, and pita bread triangles. The appetizer was delicious, but she'd need some real food when she got home. Maybe something along the lines of the savory meats and seasoned vegetables she could smell from the tables around her. For now, she sipped her wine, hoping it would give her extra strength to talk about how Marlon had broken her heart.

"He did." *Again.* "I guess he didn't really want a reconciliation between us."

It took effort to shove images of their time together into the dark recesses of her mind with her memories from fifteen years ago.

Keysha shook her head. "So what happened?"

Zerleena clenched and unclenched her teeth. "The Waves made an offer for him to return to Miami. But that's confidential information. Don't tell anyone."

"Uh, oh." Erika delivered a wealth of commentary with those two syllables.

"So that's it?" Keysha's dark eyes glowed with anger. "He comes back into your life, dredging up the past, then packs up and leaves again?"

"Wow." Erika was really accomplished with the one-syllable soundbites. "Did he at least ask if you wanted to go with him this time?"

Zerleena heard the caution in Erika's question. "He didn't ask. He just expected that I would."

Keysha gasped, then coughed as her wine entered the wrong pipe. Zerleena and Erika watched her settle herself.

"Excuse me?" Keysha wiped tears from her eyes. Sarcasm was heavy in her rhetorical question. "He expected he'd snap his fingers and you'd uproot your life for him? Typical man."

"*Some* men." Erika used a pita bread triangle to scoop some dip from her plate. Zerleena sensed her widowed friend was thinking about her beloved Manfred. They'd been so much in love and he'd died far too soon. "What did you tell him?"

"My reaction was pretty much what Key said." Zerleena nodded toward her. "Things were different when he was first drafted. We were both starting out in our careers. I thought we'd be together forever. I'd expected him to ask me to move to Miami with him then, and I would've gone. But I'm not twenty-two anymore."

Keysha grunted. "None of us are."

Zerleena continued. "I'm thirty-seven. I'm not starting out. I'm already established."

"Yes, but you're not rooted here." Erika shrugged. "Your books sell nationally. Your satellite radio show's heard everywhere and you host workshops all over the country."

Keysha narrowed her eyes. "Whose side are you on?"

Erika chuckled. "Leena's side." She turned to Zerleena seated across the table. "You're more than a friend. You're family. The thought of you leaving Brooklyn — leaving the city — makes me panic. But I want to make sure you're not holding yourself back because of past resentments." She sent Keysha a pointed look. "Or well-meaning friends."

Keysha continued to scowl. "How's she holding herself back?"

Zerleena squeezed Keysha's forearm. "It's alright, Key." Erika had taken an unexpected perspective. "I want to know."

Erika smiled. "I'm not talking professionally. Professionally, you're continuing to grow. You're expanding your audience and diversifying your revenue. But there's more to life than work. Sometimes I don't think you and Key understand that."

Keysha gasped. "Don't bring me into this."

Erika rolled her eyes. "Yes, he should've asked if you'd consider moving to Miami with him if his trade comes through. But is that teaching moment worth ending your relationship? You wouldn't have to leave Brooklyn right away. See how he handles your time apart, then make a decision. Isn't he worth taking that chance?"

"I'm scared." Zerleena stared into her half empty glass of white wine. "I don't want to go back to being in his shadow. I'm not Marlon Burress's cheerleader anymore. I'm Zerleena Chase. How do I make him understand that?"

"On some level, he does understand that." Keysha sipped her wine. "Don't you remember all the things he said when he was on Corny's show and how he called him out for attacking you?"

"Key's right." Erika inclined her head toward the other woman.

"Did it hurt you to say that?" Key asked.

"More than you'll ever know." Erika responded without looking at her. "Tell Marl what you want and what you're concerned about. At least give it some thought. We just don't want you to miss this opportunity for the wrong reasons."

And I don't want to have my heart broken a third time.

***

"Steve? What're you doing here?" Shock jolted through Marlon when he found his friend waiting with DeMarcus in the lobby of his condo building. He stepped forward to embrace the other man.

Steve returned the greeting. "I was in the neighborhood. Val says, 'Hi.'"

Marlon escorted his friends to the bank of elevators and his condo. "You happened to be in a neighborhood in another state? Did someone knock you unconscious and put you on a plane?"

Steven looked him in the eye. "Yes."

Marlon's lips curved into an appreciative smile. "They may have hit you too hard. Your sense of humor's worse now than ever before."

The trio trash talked until the elevator deposited

them on Marlon's floor. He led them into the condo's living room before getting refreshments from the kitchen. He loaded a tray with two glasses of iced tea, a bowl of roosted peanuts — he hadn't been raised in a barn — and a glass of ice water for himself.

"How long are you staying?" He carried the tray of refreshments into the living room, offering Steven and DeMarcus their drinks before setting the tray on the coffee table and taking his glass.

Steven had folded his six-foot-plus frame onto the leather sofa. "A few days."

Marlon frowned. His friend didn't have a suitcase. "You checked into a hotel? You should stay here."

"I couldn't. You're a slob, man." With his half-full glass of iced tea, Steven gestured toward DeMarcus seated in one of the two matching armchairs. "I'm staying with Julian."

Julian Guinn was DeMarcus's father. Marlon and Steven had known the elder Guinn since the trio had played for the Waves. At the time, he'd told them his son's team was his second favorite in the league behind only his beloved Monarchs. Since DeMarcus was now the Monarchs' head coach, the Guinn family was united behind the same favorite team.

Marlon gave both men a suspicious look. "What's going on?" He confronted Steven. "I'm supposed to believe you blew into Brooklyn on impulse?" He turned to DeMarcus. "And your dad's good to put him up on short notice? Don't play me. What is this?"

DeMarcus held his gaze. "It's an intervention."

His temper stirred, part impatience, part uncertainty. He'd never admit to the uncertainty. "My game's been tight."

The team had turned their season around beyond his wildest expectations. They'd fought their way to a 44-34 record and the fourth-place ranking in the Eastern Conference. If they kept that spot, they'd have home court advantage for the first round of the playoffs.

"True." DeMarcus's eyes didn't waver. "But your passion's missing."

He stood to pace. His skin was prickly. The air was draining from the room. "What're you talking about?"

"Now who's playing whom?" DeMarcus's question carried over Marlon's shoulder.

"How long have we known you?" Steven asked. "I've seen the games, Marl. You're playing some of your best ball, but you're like Millbank out there. The lights are on, but no one's home."

Marlon sent the other man a sharp look from over his shoulder. Had Steven deliberately used the words he'd spoken a couple of years ago before his friend had married Valerie? The couple had had a serious argument and ended their relationship. The separation had torn Steven up.

Sort of like this breakup with Zerleena had jacked him up.

The words were hard to speak. They made the situation real. "Leena and I've ... split-up."

DeMarcus expelled a breath. "I'm sorry, man."

"I was afraid of that." Steven's voice was heavy with empathy, as though he was remembering his own breakup. "What happened?"

Marlon drew a deep breath, trying to ease the pain in his gut. It didn't help. He didn't think talking about it would help, either, but the words wouldn't stop.

"She said I took her for granted. That I only care about myself, but she's wrong." His words sped up as he paced the width of his window. "I love her. The entire time we were apart, I couldn't get her out of my mind. And it's a thousand times worse now."

"Let's play devil's advocate," Steven suggested.

Marlon groaned. "I hate that game."

Steven ignored him. "You say you couldn't get her out of your mind the entire time you were apart. Why did you wait so long to do something about it?"

DeMarcus gestured toward Steven. "He's right. You were a serial dater: models, dancers, actresses."

Steven cocked his head. "Why didn't you ever date athletes?"

Marlon sent him a look before returning his attention to DeMarcus. "I didn't think I had the time or the energy to build a long-term relationship." He resumed his pacing. "But being with Leena's different. I want to put in the time and make the effort. There's nowhere I'd rather be, not even on the court."

Steven nodded knowingly. Marlon had a memory of the looks exchanged between Valerie and his friend. He wanted that with Zerleena for the rest of their lives.

"If you felt that way about her, why did you cut her out of your life?" DeMarcus's question distracted him from that yearning.

"That's Leena's biggest beef with you. You didn't even try to keep in touch with her. Why not?" Steven stepped forward to offer the bowl of peanuts to his friends. DeMarcus took some but Marlon declined. Steven grabbed a fistful, then returned to his seat.

Marlon turned his back to them. "I shouldn't have done that and I've apologized to her." Dear God, his voice sounded as tired and defeated as he felt.

"But why'd you do it?" DeMarcus asked.

Marlon stared through his picture window. He didn't see the spring scene unfurling beyond his condo, the buds waking on the treetops in the distance or the pedestrian laden sidewalks below. Instead he saw Zerleena, laughing with him; loving him; turning away.

"I was focused on my career." He folded his arms across his chest as though holding himself together. "I needed to be the best. My life was training, studying game film, memorizing playbooks. My goal was to be a champion. I didn't make time for love."

"But now that you think your career's over, you can make time for her?" Steven sounded dubious.

Marlon faced them. "With or without my career, I need Leena in my life."

DeMarcus nodded. "Tell her that."

Marlon scrubbed his hands over his face. "I tried. It didn't come out right."

The silence was swollen with dread. Steven spoke first. "What happened?"

Marlon looked to DeMarcus. "The Waves are considering taking me back. I asked Leena to come with me because I want a future with her."

"You're going back to the Waves?" DeMarcus's eyes stretched wide with disbelief. "Does Jack know?"

Steven held up his hand, palm out. "Marc, we'll talk about that later."

DeMarcus continued. "The Waves cut you once. Pride alone should keep you from going back."

Steven put the discussion back on track. "How did Leena respond to you?"

"Not well." Marlon winced. "She knows the Monarchs are considering extending my contract. She accused me of always thinking only of myself. She asked why she should give up everything she'd built for herself and start over in Miami when we could both build a life here."

"Marl." DeMarcus and Steven responded at the same time.

"I know. I know." He threw up his arms. "I've blown it."

Steven shook his head with a sigh. "You can't give up. She's a solid gold on your Honey Decoder Ring."

DeMarcus arched an eyebrow at Marlon. "You have a Honey Decoder Ring?"

"We're joking." Steven waved his hands, palms out. "It's an imaginary ring we use to describe relationships. Like if you're casually dating someone, you'd say the ring's green. But if the person just wants to be seen with you and spend your money, you'd say the ring's red."

"What's gold?" DeMarcus sounded genuinely interested.

"Val and Jackie would be gold." Steve referred to his wife DeMarcus's fiancée.

"And Leena," Marlon added. "She's the one for me and I've lost her. Again."

DeMarcus gave him an empathetic look. "Not necessarily—"

Marlon dropped onto his armchair, cradling his forehead in his palms. "It was hard enough convincing her to give me a second chance. She's *not* giving me a third."

"Marl. Marl." Steven's tone was urgent. "What's more important to you, living in Miami or a life with Leena?"

"A life with Leena." He didn't hesitate.

"Lead with that," Steven said.

Marlon's muscles were tight with fear. "What do I do if she won't listen?"

"Do what you always do." DeMarcus arched an eyebrow. "Keep talking."

Chapter 16

Zerleena clenched her teeth as she navigated the late Monday afternoon traffic. Vicious words she planned to hurl at Cornell when she got to his office stacked in her mind. Tightening her grip on her steering wheel, she waited for a break in the opposing traffic before navigating the left turn.

"Zerleena Chase's financial health workshops are just overpriced one-woman shows she's been trying to pass off as financial management seminars." Cornell's voice came through her cell phone, which lay on her passenger seat.

It was a struggle not to bear down on her accelerator. She rarely drove. She saved her car for longer trips and emergencies — like this one. Traffic in Brooklyn was insane and parking even crazier. But today, she didn't have the patience to wait for a bus and train to take her to Cornell's studio. Besides, walking the several city blocks to the subway might soothe her. She couldn't risk that. She wanted Cornell to witness the full force of her anger. She'd had enough of her wannabee rival.

Zerleena had been monitoring Cornell's financial management show during dinner. She should consider ending that habit. His content — everything about him — upset her appetite. She could ignore his personal barbs but today, he was attacking her workshops, which were a large part of her livelihood.

If pretending they were rivals kept him motivated, so be it. But she'd realized — far too late — that she should've taken her parents' and friends' advice and put a stop to his disparagements the minute he'd started. His childish attacks could harm her income.

"Her workshops are staged just so she could hear herself drone on and on and on and on, repeating information she puts in her books. So first of all, the information isn't even new. And it's even less accurate the second, third, fourth, and fifth times around. I mean, seriously, you can learn more about managing your finances in a junior high math class." Cornell chuckled at his own joke.

Zerleena's temper exploded. She wanted to ram those words down his throat. With an effort, she maintained the legal speed limit — just — and forced her clenched teeth apart.

"Well, folks. That was a quick two hours. This is Cornell Redd's Reddy to Earn. Thanks for tuning in." Cornell ended his Monday evening program.

Exerting great restraint, Zerleena guided her silver compact sedan into one of the few open spaces in the parking lot behind the office building that housed Cornell's radio studio. The relatively new structure stood ten stories high. Its bronze-and-black façade glinted in the streetlights flickering to life this April evening.

Zerleena slammed out of her car, stomped across the asphalt lot and into the building. After checking the business directory, she entered the elevator and pressed the button for the sixth floor. Less than two minutes later, she was standing in front of Cornell's office. She flung open the door with the full force of her fury.

Cornell started as it bounced against the wall. Eyes wide, he gaped at her. "Zerleena! If you damage my office, you're paying to fix it."

"You'd have better luck increasing your subscribers than getting me to give you a red cent." Months of remaining silent against his vitriol boiled over.

She advanced on him. Her sneakered feet were silent on the thin, blue-gray carpet. He rose behind his blond laminate desk. Zerleena narrowed her eyes, acknowledging the strategy behind his movement. He didn't want to remain seated as she and her fury loomed over him. He'd be at a disadvantage, wouldn't he?

With her peripheral vision, she noted the stunned young woman tucked behind the desk she'd strode past. She must be Cornell's production intern, Sally Bagby. She was attractive with large green eyes and a wealth of reddish-gold hair that curled past her shoulders. Odd that her desk was buried under stacks of papers while Cornell's was bare.

Cornell braced his fingertips on his desk. "What do you want?"

She couldn't answer that, not in front of witnesses.

Her impulses conflicted with her brand of encouraging people to exercise restraint and good judgement.

"You've been speaking with Carol Mart." Zerleena reined in her rage. "That's how you knew about my connection with Marlon. That's why you're disparaging my workshops."

A small smile ghosted Cornell's thin lips. "You know that I can't reveal my sources."

She tilted her head, giving Cornell a scathing scrutiny. "I can't reveal mine, either." The slight shift in his expression provided small comfort.

"What sources?" There was tension in his voice.

"People who live in glasshouses shouldn't throw stones, Corny."

His lips thinned with anger at the nickname. "What're you talking about?"

Crossing her arms over the peach-and-red floral print of her bronze sweater, Zerleena took a moment to consider her adversary. He looked fit and comfortable in a teal green sweater blazer worn over a tan jersey. Gray khakis completed the ensemble. She estimated the total cost of the garments — not including his shoes — at more than half the cost of her monthly office rent.

She jerked her chin toward him. "Those clothes look new. I'm surprised you can afford to shop like that these days."

Cornell gave an uncomfortable chuckle as he slid a quick look in Sally's direction. "Why wouldn't I be able to?"

"You had to return your advance to your last publisher when you didn't deliver the book after a year. Since then, you haven't been able to get another deal."

Blood drained from his face. "Who told you that?" he hissed. Spittal glistened on his lips.

Zerleena tsked. "We have to protect our sources. And I've got *loads* of them. *Loads.*"

Cornell shifted his glower to Sally. "Show her out." His voice was a sharp command.

Zerleena turned to the intern. "I wouldn't recommend it."

"Don't worry, I won't." Sally seemed entranced by the exchange, as though the only things missing were a bowl of popcorn and 3D glasses.

Cornell's expression darkened. "You work for *me.*"

"What you're barely paying me to be your producer isn't enough to also be your bouncer." Sally's tone was dry.

Satisfied, Zerleena turned back to her nemesis. "A second told me you didn't cancel your last workshop because you were ill. You canceled because of poor registration and you're still paying back the resort you booked a year later. Ouch."

Cornell dropped his gaze to his desk as the blood flooded back to his cheeks. His words were a low mutter. "That's enough."

But Zerleena was on a roll. "A *third* source told me those women you've been photographed with around town are paid es—"

"Stop!" The word shot from his throat like a bullet.

"That last tip I confirmed myself. The two agencies you're registered with told me you're a regular."

His blue eyes glowed with anger. "What. Do. You. Want?" The words were barely discernible through his clenched teeth.

Who's sorry now?

Zerleena settled onto one of the two blue-gray guest chairs in front of his desk. She crossed her right leg over her left, and stacked her hands on her right thigh.

She looked up, giving him a hard look to underscore the shift in power. "I want you to look into my eyes and tell me you understand if you don't stop attacking me, if you don't stop speaking my name on air *or in life*, I will ruin you." She watched his eyes shift as though he was considering his options.

There weren't any.

Cornell dropped onto his chair. "Yes."

"Say it." She smelled his defeat.

His face burned redder. "I understand that if I attack you or even say your name, you'll ruin me."

"I have the power to ruin you."

"You have the power to ruin me."

"Do you see the truth of that in my eyes?"

He held her gaze. "Yes, I do." His voice was thin. He looked and sounded like a sulky toddler in a dirty diaper.

Zerleena stood. "If my name comes up on your

show, I'll file a complaint against you with the FCC and encourage your listeners to do the same."

"For what? His face had turned beet red.

"The FCC issued your channel license for business and financial advice, not gossip. You could lose your license for violating the terms of the service you're supposed to provide." Zerleena looked around his office. "Considering this station is your only source of revenue, that could be a problem for you."

She watched the blood drain from his face before turning to leave.

"Ms. Chase?" Sally stopped her.

Zerleena looked at her. "It's Sally Bagby, isn't it?"

She face glowed. "Yes, ma'am." She shot a glance toward Cornell before turning back to Zerleena. "Do you have any open positions?"

"What?" Cornell's exclamation was a muted roar. "If you leave, don't expect me to give you a reference."

"I wouldn't ask for one. I quit." Sally collected her purse and coat.

Zerleena looked down her nose at Cornell. "And this is just the beginning, Corny."

She walked out with Sally close behind.

***

Beat the Celtics, and we'll have home court for the first round of the playoffs.

The incentive had been blaring in Marlon's head since this final regular season game had begun almost three hours ago. It was Friday night and TD Garden was rocking. His Monarchs were giving the Boston Celtics a battle.

If they beat the Celtics tonight to finish the eighty-two-game season with forty-five wins, they'd edge out their rival for the fourth-place seed in the Eastern Conference. There was just one problem: the Celtics had owned them this season. They were 0-3 in previous meetings, including a humiliating defeat on their home court.

But he believed in the Monarchs. His new team had come a long way since the season began. He'd been certain his final season in the NBA would see him miss the postseason for the first time in his career. Now he could almost feel the championship ring on his finger.

"You got this, Vinny!" He cheered the center on as he checked the shot clock again. The score was 79-76, Monarchs with six minutes left. They had fifteen seconds to make a basket and lengthen their lead against the Celtics.

Home court advantage for the first playoff series. Sweet.

Was Zerleena watching?

He shook his head.

Stay focused. Stay in the game.

But if she was watching, she must be on the edge of her seat just as everyone in TD Garden was. Just as every Monarch was — with the possible exception of Jamal.

Marlon glanced over his shoulder. Yep, just as he'd thought. With so much at stake, Jamal was sulking on his seat. Like him, the young shooting guard had clocked several minutes on the court before and after the half. He'd still seemed distracted. DeMarcus had laid into him in the locker room, and had taken him out after one play at the start of the third quarter.

"Get off your butt and cheer on the team, On-It." It had been a hard lesson for Marlon to learn. Now he was determined to evangelize his teammate.

Jamal's expression darkened. "*Jam*-On-It ain't no cheerleader, gramps."

Had any of his teammates ever taken a swing at the kid? Marlon was certain they'd at least been tempted. "It's called being a good teammate. You want that home court advantage, it's going to take all of us."

He caught the look of approval DeMarcus sent him before the coach returned his attention to the game. Shaking his head at Jamal, Marlon resumed his court-side encouragement.

The game clock was counting down, three minutes left. The aging Monarchs roster had been holding its own against the younger Celtics. But they were show-ing signs of fatigue under the seesawing lead. Boston managed to tie the game at 84 apiece. Marlon's mus-cles tightened as the sharks in Boston jerseys smelled chum in the water.

"Monarchs in four!" Marlon raised four fingers to emphasize his message they were going to hold strong for all four quarters. They couldn't ease up now.

Home court advantage. And a title. I can feel that ring.

Disaster struck. Anthony's assignment jumped for a shot. He leaped, defending the basket. He soared higher, tapping the ball off course with the tips of his fingers. Warrick snatched the rebound, claiming it for the Monarchs. But when Anthony landed on the court, his feet weren't under him.

He writhed on the floor, fighting off the pain. Marlon stood on the sideline, fearful for his teammate. A whistle called the play dead. Refs signaled an injury timeout as the Monarchs and several Celtics on the court surrounded Anthony.

DeMarcus and Oscar jogged out to help Warrick and Serge carry their injured teammate courtside.

"It's broken." Anthony gritted his teeth. "I can feel it. The same damn ankle I broke last year's broken. Again."

Shock and dismay coursed through him as Marlon imagined the weeks of rest and rehab the other man would have to endure. Even worse, the disappointment of missing the postseason. Worry over not coming back soon enough or strong enough. He knew what all of that meant for a player.

And with the team, it meant not only was the forward out for the rest of this critical game, but they'd lost him for the postseason.

Marlon leaned past DeMarcus, catching Anthony's attention. "This sucks, man, but thanks for keeping the Celtics from taking the lead."

"Yeah?" Anthony managed a smile. "Put that in a get well card."

"Coach! Coach!" Jamal's shout claimed the attention of every player, coach, and trainer around them. "I can take his spot. Lemme take it."

Anthony gave Jamal a look of disgust before the trainers helped him toward Vom 2 and the visiting team's locker room. Marlon watched them disappearing down the tunnel. That could've been any one of them. That could've been him.

"Burress." DeMarcus's voice brought Marlon back to their urgent situation. "You're in."

"What!?!" Jamal stood between DeMarcus and Marlon. His eyes were wide. His jaw had dropped. "You see all these geezers sucking wind. You're going to add another old guy to the court? They can't keep up. Put *me* in. I got this!"

DeMarcus glowered at the younger man. "I don't know what you've got. I don't think you do, either. But there's too much at stake to take a risk on you." He turned to Marlon. "Burress—"

"I know, Coach." Marlon followed his teammates onto the court. Eighty-four all. Warrick, Vincent, Barron, and Serge turned to him. "Let's not waste the sacrifice Anthony made for us."

Resolve settled onto their faces. The refs' whistle brought the game back to life. Vincent shot the ball onto the court. Warrick secured it before turning to clear a lane down court to the Celtics basket.

Marlon looked at the Celtics guard he was covering

for Anthony. The kid was at least ten years younger than him. Marlon gave him his trademark smile. Unease rippled across the baby face beneath the beard.

He sped across the court. He couldn't outrace the six-six shooting guard. The kid was probably just starting school when he'd been winning championships in the NCAA. But he'd put to use the mental skills that had persuaded Jaclyn Jones to add him to the Monarchs roster. He'd confound and confuse his opponent, keeping him off balance.

He stepped in front of Celtics guard Jaylen Brown. He caught the ball from Warrick in traffic and took it to the paint. Pumping the shot, he made a no-look pass back to the Warrick at the perimeter. The veteran guard snatched the ball and made the three-point shot in one smooth play.

87-84, Monarchs. Two minutes left.

The crowd grew silent. Tension covered the court, sucking the air from the arena.

Brown passed the ball forward to Celtics center Enes Kanter. Fall motored up court in a race against time. Vincent sprinted after him.

Son of a ... Digging deeper, Marlon spun on his heels and gave chase. He sensed the Monarchs behind him, desperate to stop the next play. The Celtics pressed them, keeping them from the ball.

Kanter took the shot from downtown. But Serge appeared from nowhere, catching it digits from the rim. Marlon slid into the space behind the Frenchman, blocking his Celtics assignment.

Serge kicked the ball forward to Warrick who passed it to Barron. Barron sprinted down court as the Celtics gave chase.

"Let's go!" DeMarcus's command overpowered the sound of sneakers squeaking against the hardwood and urged them to dig deeper.

Barron palmed the ball at the post and slammed it through the net for another two points.

89-84, Monarchs. *Home court advantage. All we need is the win.*

Monarchs fans went wild in the TD Garden. But even with less than two minutes left, the game was far from over. Five points was a tenuous lead. Garrison Mathews recovered the rebound.

Vincent got back on Kanter. Marlon stuck to Brown like a second jersey. Warrick guarded Mathews. Serge handled Robert Williams III while Barron shadowed Josh Richardson. Mathews passed the ball to Kanter who carried it over midcourt. He passed the ball around the perimeter: Brown, Williams, Mathews, and Richardson. The Monarchs blocked each of them from a clear shot to the basket. As the shot clock continued to drain, Richardson kicked the ball back to Mathews. Warrick stepped forward in a blink, stealing the ball and dribbling it back down court.

"Here!" Vincent caught the ball from Warrick. He passed it to Serge on the run.

Williams slapped the ball free from Serge and spun back toward the Monarchs basket. They had a five-point lead with seconds left to the game. They had to secure home court advantage.

But Marlon wanted the extra basket. He wasn't just looking for a wider lead. He wanted redemption for the previous debacles, especially those on his home court.

He dug deeper than he'd ever had to reach. Deeper than he'd ever needed to reach. Past the fatigue. Past the pain. He stretched beyond his legacy of trophies, records, and accolades to realize what this season of serial failures had taught him: the wins that mean the most are the ones that call upon you to give more than you think you have left to give.

Marlon ripped the ball from Williams. The game clock turned off. Monarchs got a fresh twenty-four seconds on the shot clock. He raced back to midcourt, keeping his eyes on the basket.

He pulled up short, then pitched the ball to the best player on the team.

Warrick captured the ball in one large hand. Marlon watched as the other man steadied himself far beyond the perimeter — and sent a rainbow to the net. Three points.

92-84, Monarchs. Home court advantage — and the sweetest win he'd ever had.

***

"What're you doing here?" Marlon froze as he entered his condo building and found Zerleena waiting for him in the lobby.

It was about two in the morning. Was he dreaming or was Zerleena really here?

"Congratulations." Her smile wavered. Unfolding her hands, she let her arms drop to her sides. She was wearing her silver-and-black Monarchs warmup suit. He still couldn't believe he'd bought her story about not being an NBA fan anymore.

But what was going on? Why was she here, looking as uncertain as he felt? It had been almost a month since he'd last seen her and even longer since he'd held her.

Marlon gathered his thoughts. "Thank you." He offered her a tentative smile. "But you could've just called. Why're you here, Leena?"

Zerleena looked around at the security guards on duty, doing a poor job of pretending they weren't listening to their tenant's very private conversation.

"Could we talk?" She jerked a thumb over her shoulder. "Upstairs?"

"Sure." He nodded his greetings to the two young guards as he led Zerleena to the bank of elevators.

The ride up to his floor was quiet, but comfortable. He was tired or at least he had been before he found her waiting for him. Why would she be here at two in the morning? It must mean she still had feelings for him. Right? Closing his eyes, he breathed in her soft rose scent. It stimulated and relaxed him at the same time. How was that possible?

The elevator doors opened and Marlon led her into his condo. "Can I get you something to drink?"

"No, thank you." Zerleena wrung her hands as she paced past him. "You must be tired. I'm sorry. I should've waited until the morning. I was just so anxious to speak with you."

She was rambling. That was not like her. She was making him nervous.

"Leena, what's wrong?" He dumped his gym bag and suitcase inside his entryway and crossed to her.

She walked to his living room with awkward, hesitant strides — and froze. "What happened?"

He knew what had surprised her. He'd replaced his overstuffed teal sofa and loveseat with a black leather set. Black and silver accents carried throughout the room.

Standing behind her, he smiled. "I had my car painted black, too."

She turned to him, lips parted and eyes wide. "What? Wow. What does this mean?"

Her question got to the heart of the matter. His palms were sweating. He hadn't felt as anxious during the game as he felt right now. "It means I'm staying in Brooklyn. I've asked Jett to decline the Waves's offer and to tell Jackie Jones that I'm interested in that contract extension she told me about."

"What made you change your mind?" Her voice was breathless.

"I love you too much to lose you a second time."

"I don't want you to lose you again, either. I love

you too much, but I thought you wanted to return to Miami to play with a more professional team."

Marlon drew her into his arms. "The best place for me is here with you. It's the right place for me. I've learned a lot about myself this season, like the fact that it's a lot more satisfying to bring a championship to a struggling team than it is to coast to a title with a legendary franchise."

She grinned up at him. "Well, look at you. Are you willing to end your career with a bunch of losers?"

Marlon's heart filled with so much love for her, he thought it would burst. "Your love is the only thing I never want to lose. With it, I can face whatever the future brings."

THE END

Coming Soon

Relive the *Brooklyn Monarchs*
Cinderella Season
The Brooklyn Monarchs
by Patricia Sargeant (formerly Regina Hart)
Available Now
Fast Break, Book I
Smooth Play, Book II
Keeping Score, Book III
Game Plan, Book IV
The Brooklyn Monarchs
Season 2
Game Time Decision, Book V Available Now
Her Greatest Fan, Book VI Coming Spring 2022
Watch and Learn, Book VII, Coming Summer
2022

ABOUT THE AUTHOR

Patricia Sargeant is a national best-selling, award-winning author. She writes romance as Patricia Sargeant and Regina Hart, and mysteries as Olivia Matthews. Her work has been reviewed in national publications such as *Publishers Weekly, USA Today, Kirkus Reviews, Suspense Magazine, Mystery Scene Magazine, Library Journal* and *RT Book Reviews*. Patricia was drawn to write romance because she believes love is the greatest motivation. Her mysteries put ordinary people in extraordinary situations to have them find the Hero Inside. For more information about Patricia and her work, visit PatriciaSargeant.com.

www.ingramcontent.com/pod-product-compliance
Lightning Source LLC
Chambersburg PA
CBHW021311190726
48288CB00003B/802